In Love

Rebecca James

Rebecca James

This is a work of fiction. Names, characters, places, and incidents are the product of the author's imagination, and any resemblance to actual events, locales, organizations, or persons living or dead is entirely coincidental.

In Love

Sequel to *Boys' Love*

Copyright © 2022 by Rebecca James

Cover content is for illustrative purposes only and any resemblance to persons living or dead is purely coincidental.

Cover Artist: Feddefar

Edition: 2

Edited by Royal Editing Services

All product names, logos, and brands are the property of their respective owners.

All rights reserved.

No part of this book may be reproduced or transmitted in any form or by any means without written permission from the author.

Contents

Terms Used in Series		V
Preface		1
1.	CHAPTER ONE: Rama	2
2.	CHAPTER TWO: Pravat	7
3.	CHAPTER THREE: Rama	13
4.	CHAPTER FOUR: Pravat	19
5.	CHAPTER FIVE: Rama	25
6.	CHAPTER SIX: Pravat	31
7.	CHAPTER SEVEN: Rama	36
8.	CHAPTER EIGHT: Pravat	41
9.	CHAPTER NINE: Rama	48
10.	CHAPTER TEN: Pravat	54
11.	CHAPTER ELEVEN: Rama	59
12.	CHAPTER TWELVE: Pravat	65
13.	CHAPTER THIRTEEN: Rama	72
14.	CHAPTER FOURTEEN: Pravat	78
15.	CHAPTER FIFTEEN: Rama	84

16. CHAPTER SIXTEEN: Lin — 90
17. CHAPTER SEVENTEEN: Pravat — 95
18. CHAPTER EIGHTEEN: Rama — 100
19. CHAPTER NINETEEN: Pravat — 108
20. CHAPTER TWENTY: Rama — 113
21. CHAPTER TWENTY-ONE: Pravat — 117
22. CHAPTER TWENTY-TWO: Rama — 121
23. CHAPTER TWENTY-THREE: Pravat — 129
24. CHAPTER TWENTY-FOUR: Rama — 133
25. CHAPTER TWENTY-FIVE: Pravat — 138
26. CHAPTER TWENTY-SIX: Rama — 146
27. CHAPTER TWENTY-SEVEN: Rama — 151
28. CHAPTER TWENTY-EIGHT: Pravat — 156
29. CHAPTER TWENTY-NINE: Rama — 160
30. CHAPTER THIRTY: Pravat — 166
31. CHAPTER THIRTY-ONE: Rama — 173
32. CHAPTER THIRTY-TWO: Rama — 180

Acknowledgements — 186

Also By Rebecca James — 187

Terms Used in Series

Auntie and Uncle: Used for an older woman or older man in an affectionate respect.

BTS (when talking about video clips): Stands for "behind the scenes."

BTS (Bangtan Sonyeondan): Popular Korean KPop group.

BTS Skytrain: Bangkok's mass transit system.

Boys' Love (abbr. bl or BL and sometimes written as *boyslove*, also called *yaoi*): A genre of fiction originating in Japan that features homoerotic relationships between men. Unfortunately, some of the bl industry is reported to be quite caustic, with heavy restrictions on the actors, including dating bans. While I make note of this in the book, I've chosen to have Rama and Pravat work for a less restrictive company.

Congee (or Jok): Rice boiled down until it's like a porridge, usually with a bone broth. Different spices and foods are added.

Faculty: In Thailand, the colleges are divided into faculties of study.

Fanmeets: When actors meet up with their fans at a designated place and sign autographs, answer questions, etc.

Fanservice (or fan service): Contractual agreement to act as though possibly in a relationship with shipped partner for all work-related events.

Farang: Thai word for Caucasian.

"Husband" and "Wife": Thai culture, many men in gay relationships call each other the equivalent of "ma" and "pa" in reference to the sexual position they prefer in the relationship. According to some sources, the words used are better translated as "hubby" and "wifey" and are not meant to be serious or offensive.

Irl: slang abbreviation for "in real life" as opposed to on the show.

Khao Soi: Northern Thai curry noodle soup.

Khao Tom: A popular Thai rice soup.

Khun or Khun P: Used for Mr. and Mrs.—a more respectful address for someone older.

Lakorn: A Thai soap opera.

LINE IDs: LINE is a popular message app in Thailand with cute stickers. A person's ID can be shared without giving out a phone number.

Motosai: Motorcycle; a thai motorbike taxi.

NC scenes: NC is a rating that stands for No Children. NC 17+, NC 18+, NC 21+. Boys' love series with these ratings have content unsuitable for children under these ages.

"Na, na, na?": Begging *please*.

Nong: Respectful address for a younger person in one's age group.

Nong Sau: Little Sister.

P': (P'Name. Pronounced "Pee."): Respectful address for an older person of one's age group.

Sawasdee: Hello or goodbye. Sometimes shortened to "Wadee." Add "kha" for female speaking or "khap" for male (polite address).

Senior: Respectful address to an older person—even by just a year or two. It might be shocking to learn of upper and lower classmates not in the same year.

Ship: Short for relationship. When fans and/or production companies couple the actors as a romantic pair.

Ship name: Fans put the names of the two actors together to form one name for their ship. The "dominant" partner's name goes first. Sometimes each name is whole, such as with ThornPhai, and others it is blended, such as with Pravma (Pravat and Rama from previous books).

Ship work: A couple actively working on their ship to keep it relevant and believable, etc.

Siam Paragon: A massive mall in Bangkok, Thailand.

Singha: A popular Thai beer.

Skinship: (wordplay on "skin" and "kinship.") Feelings of affection between two people brought on by hugging, touching, cuddling, and other physical contact. Skinship is encouraged between actors during bl workshops to develop closeness between those who are playing couples.

Sniff kiss: A type of kiss in Thailand generally accepted in public. Rather than touching lips, the sniff kiss is when a person puts their nose to someone's cheek and inhales. The deeper the inhale, the stronger the affection.

Songkran: the Thai new year, which is celebrated April 13-15.

Stan: a very zealous fan of something or someone. Also used as a verb for really liking something/someone, as in "I stan this ship."

SuSu: means "fighting" as in encouragement to keep going.

Thai nicknames: many Thai nicknames are English words or sound like English words, all chosen for their meaning and meant to keep jealous spirits away. Examples: Bean, Book, Bank, Milk, Light, Bum, Ply, Ice, Fah.

Thai surnames: In Thailand, no surname is permitted to be alike. The surnames used in this novel are from either name generators or generations-old family names. My apologies for any mistakes made there.

Troll: Someone who purposely starts trouble on the internet.

Uncle: Used for an older man in an affectionate respect.

Wai: (pronounced "why"): A gesture of respect when greeting. Press palms together and bow head.

Workshop: Rehearsal for the series. Often, skinship is practiced.

Y-girl: Yaoi girl.

Y-couple: a term fashioned from the Japanese word Yaoi, a genre of male/male romance, indicating an MM relationship. The term Y-couple is used in this book referring to a couple starring in a boys' love drama together.

Yah: Grandmother on the father's side.

Yaoi: a genre of fictional media originating in Japan that features homo-erotic relationships between male characters. (Also known as boys' love or bl.)

Preface

Dear Reader,

This book is the sequel to *Boys' Love*. Reading book one before the sequel is strongly advised.

Warning: This book deals with trauma from the past sexual abuse of a minor.

As this book is set in Thailand, please check out the list of terms used.

CHAPTER ONE: Rama

♥

"Cut!" The director's voice blasts from the speaker, calling an end to the scene. Immediately, Mint pushes Two away from him, knocking the smaller man off balance, so that he has to steady himself with a hand on the wall. Seconds before, the two men were the picture of romantic love, staring soulfully into each other's eyes, lips nearly touching, but now they stare balefully at each other, their mouths drawn up in sneers of dislike.

This abrupt contrast is something I've grown used to over the past few weeks of filming the sequel to *My Doctor, My Love*, the boys' love drama that tossed me into the limelight last year as one half of the popular Y-couple adoring fans have dubbed *Pravma*.

Catching the eye of Pravat, the other half of that couple, I raise a brow at him, and he gives me a subtle eye roll in agreement that Mint and Two are exhausting.

Tall and handsome with cut cheekbones, narrow eyes, and a sunny smile that has made my heart do crazy things since day one—even though he's a man and I've never been interested in men-Pravat Benjawan has become the center of my universe.

I might be worried about it if I wasn't so exhausted. Our filming schedule is brutal.

Due to numerous hold-ups, neither of us has slept in the last thirty-six hours other than a quick catnap here and there between scenes. Yesterday I spent three hours filming a fifteen-second clip where all I did was button my shirt and cuffs. By the time we got it right, I felt like I put in twelve hours of hard labor.

Nahm, our producer Tida's assistant, hands me a cup of steaming coffee, and I take a sip, mentally preparing myself for my next scene, which is with Mint.

On the surface, Mint's an okay guy, but the blatant homophobia he lets loose after every love scene with Two grates on my nerves. It's as though he has to remind everyone that he's only in this for the money and the last thing he wants to be doing is kissing a guy. The first time he wiped his mouth and made a face after a kissing scene, I was shocked and asked Pravat why in the world someone who feels that way would want to star in dramas that pair men together romantically.

"Because nothing can launch a guy's career as quickly as a bl drama," Pravat answered, adding with a small smile, "No one should know that better than you, P'Rama. There will always be actors like Mint, only in it for the glory it can bring."

Pravat's been in the boys' love industry for a while now and is used to its harsher side. Nearly black-listed when his previous co-star outed him as gay, he considers himself fortunate that Hearts Productions took a chance on him with *My Doctor, My Love*, our first series together. He's never confirmed his sexuality, though. That would amount to career suicide in this industry where producers prefer their actors to be straight. They say it causes more sexual tension and less drama, but someone only needs to look at Mint and Two to see it's a disaster waiting to happen. Mint always leaves a good two feet of space between them, even when they're filming a kiss, and his animosity spurs a reaction in Two every time, inevitably provoking an argument. I've heard Tida claim this animosity between them is why their fanservice is so good, but all it's going to take is one caustic look caught on camera, and it will all blow up in their faces.

A member of the crew takes my empty coffee cup from my hand, and I murmur a thank you, which earns me a deep blush from the girl. I search out Pravat again, who appears to be sleeping standing up, leaning against the wall with his eyes closed as the crew prepares for the next scene.

I cross the room and gently rest my hand on his arm, meeting those dark eyes when they open. I'm rewarded with a disarming smile and, lightly, I squeeze his warm flesh with my fingers before letting go.

Our lives are made of small moments like this. If Tida were to find out we're together, she could claim breach of contract and fire us. More likely, she'd keep us under constant supervision until the series finishes airing, and Pravat and I would be lucky if we got to touch at all off camera for the next few months.

Mint shoots me a cocky smile as he passes, and I follow him to take my place on set.

I miss Aran and Tait, the actors who played the secondary couple in season one. They've started their own spin-off series, and I miss their easy companionship, especially when watching Mint and Two's behavior.

Mint and I shoot the scene in four takes, and before Mint walks away, he gives me a bro-slap on the shoulder.

Standing from the couch where I'd been sitting during the scene, I teeter slightly, dizzy from lack of sleep and skipping lunch. A hand clasps my elbow, and I turn to find Pravat's face only inches from mine. The scent of him—something warm and spicy that I've grown addicted to over the past year and a half—envelopes me, soothing my frayed nerves at the same time it makes my heart beat faster.

"One last scene and Maha says we can quit for the day," he tells me, easing away when I'm steady on my feet.

I nod, wondering what day it even *is*.

Unfortunately, I'm not as lucky with the next scene as I was with the last, my tongue refusing to wrap around my lines and forcing me to do multiple takes of the same damned sentence with its scrutinizing close-up until I think my head's going to explode with the tension building inside it.

"Cut!" Maha says when I flub up the line yet again. "Rama, what can we do to help you get through this?" he asks. The man has the patience of Job.

"Twenty-four hours of sleep might do it," I mumble, rubbing at my eyes only to earn a deep sigh from the makeup artist, who rushes in to fix what I smeared with my fingers.

A member of the crew hands me a fresh cup of coffee. I take a sip, then jerk when the hot liquid scalds my tongue. I wind up spilling it on my hand and the floor. This instigates a flurry of activity around me, and the poor girl who brought me the coffee is taken to task by Maha. She leaves the room in tears.

Rattled, I'm close to tears myself, and I struggle to find the energy I need to finish the scene. Feeling Pravat's gaze on me, I meet it and take a deep breath, releasing some of my frustration and exhaustion with it, centering myself.

When Nahm finishes applying ice to my hand, we try the scene again. And again—until even Maha's ready to scrap the whole thing and start over tomorrow. But I refuse to quit.

Pravat patiently goes through take after take with me until I finally get it right and we're able to move on. By the time filming wraps up, the sun is peeking over the horizon, bringing a rosy hue to downtown Bangkok.

Knowing I have to be ready to film again in only a few short hours, I drop onto the couch without preamble and curl up, almost immediately sinking into a deep sleep. At some point, when my consciousness briefly rises to the surface, I'm aware of a warm body pressed against mine under a blanket before exhaustion tugs me under again.

CHAPTER TWO:

Pravat

♥

Since we started filming *More Love*, the negative postings about me on popular bl drama sites have increased, and I don't have to think too deeply about it to know who is behind them. Undoubtedly jealous of my success with the new series, my ex-co-star, Preed, is doubling his efforts to ruin me in this business. Normally, I'd ignore his petty attempts, but lately they've involved Rama, too, and I won't tolerate anyone hurting Rama.

Currently, the bl gossip sites are rife with rumors that Rama and I are involved. Although the idea of us as a couple in real life is popular with fans, the speculation may ruin our chances of work when this series ends. We won't always be paired together, and the idea that we only come as a pair won't be good for our careers. And unlike Rama, who comes from a rich family, I need mine.

Considering all of this, I'm not too surprised when Tida asks to see me in her office one morning when I arrive on set early. She hired me when no one else would, choosing to believe in my innocence over Preed's allegations that I'm gay and sexually harassed him on set.

Shame fills me that I've brought her trouble, even though I realize I have no control over what Preed does.

Situated at the far corner of the upper floor of the building that houses Hearts Productions, Tida's spacious office is filled with floor-to-ceiling photos of her leading men. An eight-by-ten of Rama and me hangs directly above her head. It's become a well-known image: Me lifting Rama off his feet, my hands linked beneath his ass as he looks down into my eyes, a beatific smile on his face and the ocean as our backdrop.

"Good morning, Pravat." Tida's bright yellow blouse with red poppies printed on it serves as a spot of warmth against the dreary rain beating against the large plate-glass window behind her.

"Sawasdee khrap," I greet her, giving the wai before sitting in the chair across from her desk.

Adjusting her tortoiseshell glasses, Tida gets right to the point. "I'm sure you've seen the recent postings about you and Rama."

I nod. "I'm sorry."

She holds up her hand. "Not your fault. I've spoken with your agent, and we agree that something needs to be done to curb these rumors. So, I've arranged for the daughter of a good friend to be photographed with you." She slides a photo across her desk of a pretty girl around my age. "Her name is Lin. No formal statement will be made. You will simply spend time with her and let the gossip take its course."

Since I never replied to Preed's accusations, planting the seed that I may have a girlfriend is an excellent counter-attack. This is not a farce I want to participate in, but I feel I owe it to Tida for all she's done for me.

Tida studies my face for so long, I begin to wonder if she knows the truth. "Don't worry, this will be subtle," she finally says, breaking the tension. "A candid photo of you and Lin here and there—just enough to curb the rumors. If we go overboard, no one will believe it. You don't have to say a word, just go along."

I murmur my assent, pushing the photo of Lin back to her. There's nothing else I can do. Playing straight to the public has always been a part of my work. A gay man playing a straight man playing a gay man—now there's a conundrum for you.

"Lin will be by the studio later today to introduce herself, then the two of you will have dinner together. I've arranged for a photographer to take some candid shots that we'll leak to the press. How are you and Rama doing?"

The abrupt change of topic takes me off guard, and, for a moment, I think she's asking about our relationship.

"I know you haven't gotten much sleep lately," she prompts.

Get a grip, Pravat. "We're doing okay. It's all part of it," I say.

She nods and after chatting a moment longer about upcoming scenes, she dismisses me.

Back in the common room, I find Rama lying on a quilt on the floor, his script covering his face, undoubtedly catching a nap before our scene together. My eyes roam from his stockinged feet up his long jean-clad legs to his narrow chest rising and falling rhythmically in sleep beneath a blue T-shirt printed with the word *Bae* in white. I want to lift the script from his face and kiss him awake; instead, I cross the room and pour myself a cup of coffee from the carafe on the table. It's tempting to grab a donut from the box, too, but I have to stay in shape for the upcoming NC scenes we'll be filming. *More Love* pushes the envelope in that respect even more than its prequel did. Since Tida's anxious to get these scenes filmed so they can be included in the trailer, for the next month or so Rama and I—and to a lesser extent Mint and Two—will have our shirts off more than we'll have them on.

As I have a couple of scenes without Rama this morning, I leave him sleeping and join the crew on a lower floor that's been set up as the hospital where my character, Kusa, does his internship.

Two makes a brief appearance in the first scene, so he's waiting around when I get down there.

"Everything good?" I ask.

"Sure, why?"

I shrug. "I'd imagine Mint would get to you after awhile."

Two scowls. "Believe me, I don't want to be that close to him anymore than he wants to be to me. I envy your relationship with Rama. It seems so easy. Honestly, I thought Rama was a snob when I first met him, but around you he's a completely different person."

His words creep over me, wrapping around my heart and squeezing, and I fight to withhold the silly smile trying to form on my lips.

"Yeah, well, we got lucky. It's not always that way with your co-star."

Two becomes serious. "I heard about what happened with your last drama. Preed's such a dick. I starred a small roll in *Love Soup*, and the way he treated his co-star in that was abysmal. I don't think that guy's been in anything else since."

Maha strides in the door and a hush falls over the room.

Filming takes longer than expected due to a camera malfunction, and by the time we wrap up, it's nearly four o'clock in the afternoon. Rama is still on the floor where he was when I left, but he's awake now, studying his script.

"Have a good nap?" I ask, squatting beside him.

He smiles, lighting up his dark eyes.

"I got at least an hour of sleep before Nahm woke me with a revision to our scene," he says. "Have you seen it?"

Shaking my head, I drop to my ass on the quilt, the warmth of his body leaking into mine as our sides touch. I treasure moments like these, even more so than our intimate touches on camera. I long for the day we have time to explore our relationship in private.

Rama and I run through the scene together several times before Maha calls us to block it out. It takes only seconds to click into our roles these days, and we don't have any trouble once the cameras start rolling.

It's past eight o'clock when we finally break for the day, and I'm exhausted.

As the crew moves equipment, Rama stretches and asks me, "Do you want to grab something to eat?"

I'm about to suggest we pick something up and take it to my place when a light touch on my arm brings me around to face a pretty girl around my age. There's something familiar about her.

"Pravat? Hi, I'm Lin. P'Tida told me I could find you here."

I completely forgot about my talk with Tida earlier.

"Hi. Have you been waiting long?"

She shakes her head, two dimples appearing in her cheeks when she smiles. "Not that long. I've been watching you film. You two are great together. I can see why there's so much speculation about the two of you." Her eyes go to Rama behind me, and I hurry to introduce them.

"Lin is the daughter of a friend of Tida's. We, uh, we're having dinner together tonight," I say.

Rama's expression doesn't change, but I know he's wondering. I want to ask him to join us, but I can't do that. It has to be Lin and me alone so the photos can be taken.

"I'll see you tomorrow," I tell him, guilt filling me at the brief look of confusion in Rama's eyes before he nods and gives Lin a polite wai before walking away.

I plan to tell him what's going on, of course, but I can hardly do it here in the studio with so many people around us.

"Shall we go?" I ask Lin, steering her toward the door. I swear I can feel Rama's eyes on my back as we leave.

CHAPTER THREE: Rama

♥

"Rama." My sister, Chinda, sinks onto the living room couch beside me and shoves her iPad in my face. "Who is his girl with Pravat?"

I glance at the photo of Pravat and Lin walking in downtown Bangkok, his head tilted slightly to the side as though listening to what she's saying.

I return my attention to my laptop. "Some daughter of a friend of P'Tida's."

"They look...comfortable together."

I shrug. The picture makes me want to grab Chinda's iPad and throw it across the room.

"Well, people are talking about them, especially after seeing this shot." Again, she shoves her iPad into my line of vision.

This photo is of Lin and Pravat sitting very close, smiling at each other over dinner at a sushi bar.

"Fans will make a big deal over anything, you know that," I say, pushing her arm away.

"Yeah, but..." She pauses, biting her lip and looking at me askance. "I thought you and Pravat were together."

"Why would you think that?"

"Aren't you?" she asks pointedly.

"Chinda, you know this is an act all bl actors perform."

"Some much better than others," Chinda says with a stubborn lift of her chin.

"Thank you," I say before going back to the document my father asked me to look over. I have no idea what the last three paragraphs said.

Punching me in the arm hard enough to make me glare at her, Chinda scowls back at me, but I've been perfecting mine for a lot longer and easily win.

She looks away but mutters, "You can deny it all you want, but I know there's more than friendship between the two of you. It's okay. I get it. You aren't in a position to share." She holds up a hand to stop my protest. "But when you are, I expect details." She gets up and leaves the room.

When I hear her bedroom door click shut behind her, I take out my phone and bring up a popular bl fan site. The pictures of Pravat with Lin are all over the front page, most with caustic comments that make me feel a little sorry for Lin, but some with interested speculation about the two as a couple.

Army_sugalover: I knew Pravat wasn't gay! Those were all rumors made up by Preed.

Minhosgrl2011: They look so good together. <3 I'm so glad that he's found someone. He deserves all the happiness in the world.

Scowling, I scroll through similar comments until my phone vibrates in my hand. Seeing Pravat's name on the screen, I attempt to sound cheerful as I answer.

"Hello?"

"Hey. Enjoying your morning off?"

"Yeah. I hope you aren't working too hard without me." *What time did you go to bed? Were you alone?*

I don't know why I'm thinking this way. I know that Pravat's gay.

"Not really. We wrapped the scene where the patient dies, then I took a nap in one of the back rooms."

"It go okay?" I've learned the hard way how much emotional scenes can take out of an actor.

"Yeah. I'm just waiting for them to call me for my scene with Two and Mint."

I can't help but chuckle. "Have fun with that."

Pravat laughs with me, then draws in a breath. "Have you, uh, seen the pictures circulating?"

"Of you and Lin? Yes. The fans are being hard on your friend."

"It's to be expected. And she isn't exactly my friend, although she's very nice."

I wait for him to explain, the pause extending so long I begin to think he's not going to.

But then he says, "P'Tida wants people to think Lin and I are dating."

I freeze. "What? Why?"

"To combat the rumors that you and I are together."

Ah. That never occurred to me. "How is disappointing the majority of our fans better?" I ask.

"You know that part of the allure of bl is the idea of straight men getting intimate with each other. The rumors that I'm gay ruin that.

As soon as one of us is paired with someone else in another drama, they'll forget all about *Pravma*, anyway."

I don't like this, but what can I do about it? Then I realize what a selfish prick I'm being. It will be much better for Pravat if the rumors Preed is spreading about him are defused.

Pravat sighs and, lowering his voice, says, "I want to be with you."

The tingling sensation in my groin that his tone elicits zips upward to collide with the butterflies in my stomach. I can't believe what this man does to me.

"Me, too," I say.

A beep alerts me that someone's calling on the other line.

"I have to go," I tell Pravat. "I'll be there soon."

I click over and answer.

"Hey, Rama. It's Alex."

Alex is my cousin Pete's boyfriend. He doesn't normally call me, so I'm kind of surprised. "Hey. Is Pete okay?"

"Yeah, of course. How are you doing?"

I'm unsure if he's just making conversation or really wanting to know how I've been since the breakdown I suffered when I visited them last summer. "I'm doing well, thanks."

"I'm glad. We've been worried about you. Listen, I'm sorry this is kind of rushed, but I wanted to let you and your dad and sister know that Pete and I are making wedding plans. We've decided to have a ceremony there in Thailand next March."

Smiling, I lean back on the couch. Alex and Pete have been together for a long time and everyone's been wondering when they were going to take the next step. "That's great!"

"Yeah, we're excited. It won't be legal there, of course. We'll do that here with my family. But we want to have a ceremony there, too, so all your relatives can attend. Plus, we can have our honeymoon there."

"Sounds like an awesome plan. Uh, not that I don't want to talk to you, but why isn't Pete calling? I haven't heard from him in a while." *Not since I told him about our Aunt Sunnee and what she did to me.*

A long silence ensues that strengthens the suspicion that's been niggling at the back of my brain lately.

"He doesn't believe me," I say quietly.

"It's not that," Alex hurries to say. "It's just hard for him."

Suddenly angry, I snap back, "Don't you think it was hard for me all those years living with the secret that our aunt molested me?"

"I'm sorry, Rama," Alex says softly. Am I imagining the patronizing tone? "Give him some time, okay? He's trying to deal with it. It was a lot to take in, and now, with the wedding plans, he has a lot on his mind."

A choked noise rises from my throat. "Well, excuse me if I'm not very sympathetic!"

My sister appears in the doorway, and it's only then that I realize I've been shouting. Lowering my voice, I say, "I wouldn't lie about something like that."

"Of course you wouldn't, Rama," Alex says. "Listen, I hate to cut this short, especially when you're upset, but I'm at the theater and have some people waiting for me. Would you tell Korn and Chinda about our plans? I'll get back with you on the particulars as the day gets closer. And take care, man."

He disconnects, leaving me staring at the phone. When I raise my eyes, Chinda is no longer in the doorway.

I breathe in deeply and then slowly let it out, as my therapist has encouraged me to do when the memories start creeping in.

In. Out. In. Out.

Aunt Sunnee's quiet whisper in the darkness. "Kwang."

In. Out. In. Out.

The weight of her hand on my arm and the rustle of the sheets as the bed dips.

My breaths get faster. *In. Out. In. Out.*

The moment I realize what is happening.

Springing to my feet, I begin pacing the room, agitated, my body feeling too large for my clothing but my skin too tight to contain the horrible guilt rising within me that somehow, *somehow*, I was to blame.

Right now, with this awful weight crushing my chest, all I can think is that I want Pravat. Grabbing my keys with shaking fingers, I bolt for the door.

CHAPTER FOUR: Pravat

♥

Rama bursts into the studio, eyes nervously searching the common room until they land on me where I'm sitting going over recent changes in the script with Maha. Shoving his trembling hands into his pockets, he shifts awkwardly from one foot to the other.

Alarmed, I rise from the couch, saying, "Excuse me, P'Maha," and walk over to Rama.

"Are you all ri—*oof*!"

Rama's embrace knocks me back a step. Feeling his heart hammering against my chest, I tentatively bring my hand to the back of his head, holding his face to my neck. With the curious gazes of cast and crew on us, I maneuver him into the nearest room where two tech guys look up from a tangle of cords they're unraveling before quickly exiting, closing the door behind them.

"What's happened?" I ask. I haven't seen him this upset for months, and I'm worried.

"It's silly. I'm sorry." His expression is tight.

"Shh, it's not silly." Tugging him to a chair, I pull him onto my lap, and he curls into me like it's where he's wanted to be all along. I stroke his soft hair. "Tell me what's wrong."

"Alex called." Rama's long fingers curl into my shirt.

"Pete's boyfriend?"

I got to know the two men a little when Rama stayed with them earlier in the year. Both seemed to be nice guys who were genuinely concerned about Rama when he had his breakdown while visiting them.

"Did he say something to upset you?" I ask.

"He called to tell me he and Pete are getting married here next March."

I frown, unsure why that news would upset Rama, who always seemed fine with his cousin and his boyfriend.

"I thought it was weird that Pete wasn't calling me himself," Rama explains before I can ask. "He doesn't want to talk to me because he thinks I'm lying about what Aunt Sunnee did to me."

My hand stills in Rama's hair. "Alex said that?"

"No. He said Pete's having trouble processing it," Rama answers bitterly, "but that's what it amounts to. He had Alex call me because he didn't want to talk to me himself."

Pressing my lips to his head, I tighten my hold on him. The skinship necessary to play our roles has blossomed over the last year into a tactile affection that I've never experienced with anyone before, and with Rama this upset, I need to be near him. I know this is why he came early to seek me out.

"I'm sorry. I'm sure that hurts," I say quietly, while, inside, I'm raging at Pete.

"Why would he believe her over me? Why would I lie about something like that?" Rama asks, raw hurt thickening his voice.

"I'm sure once he's had time to digest everything, the two of you will talk things out," I say.

Sitting up, Rama stares at me.

"Why do I feel like the villain in this?" he asks.

"It's not fair," I agree.

Searching my eyes, he appears to deflate before saying, "Do you...think what happened was somehow my fault?"

"No! No, it wasn't your fault, Rama. Put that out of your mind." Cupping his face in my hands, I say emphatically, "You are not to blame."

With a soft sigh, Rama returns his head to my shoulder. "Pah was the one I was so afraid to tell. I didn't expect Pete to act this way."

"Pete's confused. He'll come around."

After a few minutes of quiet, Rama stirs and moves off my lap, leaving me suddenly cold.

"I'm going to wash my face. I'll meet you in the common room," he tells me.

I rise and straighten out my clothing. When I leave the room, Tida approaches me looking concerned.

"Everything all right?"

I nod. The cast and crew all know Rama went through something traumatic during the hiatus between seasons of the series, although they have no idea what it was. I'm sure they're all concerned after seeing Rama so upset. Looking around, I give them all a reassuring smile. I'm surprised to spot Lin sitting at one of the tables, a highlighter in her hand and a pile of papers in front of her. She returns my smile before ducking her head and getting back to whatever she's doing.

Following my gaze, Tida explains, "I've employed Lin. It can only help to have her in some of the behind-the-scenes footage."

I suppose that's true.

Rama returns to the room, face freshly washed and hair combed back from his patrician face. Mint grabs his arm before he can head my way, and I hear him say, "We need to run through our lines for our scene." *Uh oh. The last thing Rama needs right now is to deal with Mint.*

Quickly approaching them, I say, "Rama and I need to rehearse. Our scene is first."

"What the hell were you two doing in there with the door closed so long if you weren't rehearsing?" Mint looks between us, obviously annoyed.

I want to retort that we were fucking, just to see the shock and disgust on his face, but I can't even joke about that. It's bad enough he makes it sound like we've done something wrong just by being alone in a room together.

Glaring at Mint in answer, I tug Rama to the far corner of the room. The scene we're filming today is an emotional one. I'm not sure if that's a good or a bad thing for Rama right now. He might break down. When we run through the lines, I can feel him holding back, and, unfortunately, an hour later in front of the cameras, he does exactly as I feared and bursts into tears.

"Cut!" Maha calls. "Stand by, everybody. Rama, take a minute." He busies himself while I sit with Rama, so close our thighs press together.

"I'm sorry," Rama says, wiping his face.

"It's okay. Maybe you just needed to let it out." I hand him a tissue from the box on the table. Rama nods miserably, and we sit quietly for a few moments until Maha approaches again.

"Okay?"

"Yeah. Sorry," Rama apologizes again.

"Better too much emotion than none at all," Maha says.

Rama's better after that, and we move on, but I can see he's upset with himself. No one's harder on Rama Sathianthai than Rama Sathianthai.

It's three in the afternoon when we finish filming and collapse onto one of the couches. Someone hands us each a bottle of water and a snack.

"Thanks."

"You're welcome. Looks like you're worn out."

Looking up, I see its Lin.

"Anything else I can get you?"

Shaking my head, I open my bag of seaweed chips. "No, thanks."

"Your ex-co-star's on a rampage on Twitter," Lin says, perching on the arm of the sofa.

Rama's face instantly becomes a black cloud. "That asshole."

"He's saying there's no way you could be with a woman."

I wish Lin would stop, but she doesn't.

"You have many fans defending you, though, some outright calling Preed a liar. Others say it's none of his business either way. The whole thing isn't making him look good."

"His jealously will be his downfall eventually," Rama mutters. After a moment, I rescue his bag of chips from falling from his lap to the floor when he sinks farther into the couch, arms crossed over his chest and eyes closed.

"He's saying he'll prove you and Rama are together," Lin whispers to me.

Tired, I rub my eyes. "He can't, so I'm not worried about it." Not because it isn't true, as Lin should think is my meaning, but because anything that Preed might bring up as proof can easily be explained away as the normal closeness many bl actors display in the middle of filming a series. "He's just blowing hot air."

Wanting to get rid of her, I place the chips on the floor and stretch out, head on Rama's lap. "I think I'll take a quick nap, too."

The good thing about being exhausted is it doesn't leave much time for worry. I'm asleep before I can put together another thought or notice when Lin walks away.

CHAPTER FIVE: Rama

♥

I spend the night at Pravat's, something I've started doing a lot since he lives much closer to the studio than I do. That's not the only reason, of course. Now that we've agreed our relationship will be changing in the near future, we want to be alone as much as possible, even if we do spend the majority of that time sleeping. We're always so exhausted after a day's work, we fall into bed as soon as we shower, quickly losing consciousness in each other's arms. I have to admit I enjoy it a lot. I never slept with any of the women I dated. I never wanted to.

Although I'm comfortable and happy to have Pravat's arms wrapped around me, I don't fall asleep right away. I can't stop thinking about Pete. Close in age, we've always been tight, even after he and his family moved to America. His doubt in me cuts deep.

Beside me, Pravat quietly snores, one long, tan leg thrown over mine and a hunk of damp hair tumbling over his forehead. My cock stirs in my cotton sleep pants. I want him. But, unfortunately, I have no idea how to proceed physically. He's a man, after all. Also, I'm leery of taking the next step when I've so recently torn open the old wounds concerning my aunt. Today's mini breakdown proved that I haven't progressed as much as I would like to think. If I give into my desire to take things further now, I might make a mistake that costs us our careers and even our relationship. Better to wait for the series to be over to deepen our relationship behind closed doors. Being with him like this now is enough.

Besides, Pravat's got enough worries with the rumors that fucker Preed is spreading. I completely understand why Tida's doing damage control by bringing Lin into the mix, although I don't like it. And now Lin's at the studio, everywhere I turn, it seems like. I know it doesn't make sense for me to be jealous since Pravat isn't into women at all, but I can't help it. Maybe he just *thinks* he's not into them. I know it's selfish, but I want to be the only person linked with him as his love interest. I've never been the jealous type, but with Pravat, all I see is green.

Sighing, I roll to my side and stare out the window at the reflection of lights and nearby buildings glittering on the dark waters of the Chao Phraya River. High above, a three-quarter moon hangs in the sky, the occasional cloud marring its surface. When I was little, I used to talk to the moon through the open curtains while lying in bed at night. Fancifully, I would ask it to help me with problems—usually how to get out of some trouble I got into by not minding Pah. For years I asked it to bring Mah back.

Now I whisper to it, "Take these memories away."

Pravat grunts and scoots closer to me, falling into a deep, even breathing pattern once he's settled, his body a warm fire at my back. I remember the day I first visited him and envisioned him lying with a lover in front of this view of the river and city. Inching back a little,

I mold myself to him, and when his arm comes up to encircle me, I suddenly feel like crying.

Eventually, cheeks wet, I fall asleep with his warm breath on my nape.

·♥·♥·♥·♥·♥·

The next thing I know, light is pouring through the window and my cell phone is buzzing on the floor beside the bed. Scooping it up, I mumble something unintelligible.

"Rama?" a familiar voice breaks into my grogginess. Suddenly, I'm fully awake, gripping the phone.

"Rama. It's Aunt Sunnee."

I can barely breathe. I haven't talked to her in years. *Why is she calling me?*

Voice hardening, she says, "Rama, I know you're there. I can hear you breathing. You don't have to speak, just listen. This is getting out of hand. With Pete's wedding coming up, you've put me in a very uncomfortable situation. Your father isn't speaking to me, and everyone else is asking questions. You need to tell the truth." When I don't reply, she softens her tone. "Whatever it is you think you remember isn't real. You know I'd never hurt you, Kwang."

As though electrified, I suck in a breath and shout, "Don't call me that!" Throwing the phone across the room, I leap out of bed and stare down at where it rests on the carpet like it's a venomous snake.

Her tinny voice is clear. "Bah! Why are you spreading these vicious lies about me? You have to repair the damage you've done. Tell Korn the truth!"

"I did tell him the truth!" I yell at the phone before running into the bathroom and slamming the door. Over my heavy breathing, I hear Pravat get out of bed and then the low murmur of his voice.

Realizing he's talking to my aunt and unable to stand the thought, I climb into the tub to escape, sitting on the cold porcelain and then turning on the water to drown out the sound.

Frigid jets hit my skin like needles as I hide my face in my hands and give into the tears, asking myself over and over again why this happened to me. What did I do to deserve it? What did I do all those years ago to draw my aunt's attention? And how can she deny it so confidently now? To *me*? I was there. I saw…I felt…

Bile rises in my throat and I retch, but there's nothing in my stomach to throw up. I'm shaking from more than the cold. I *hurt*, and it feels good because maybe I deserve it.

Beneath the sound of the shower and my crying and retching, I hear the doorknob rattle. Pravat calls my name. When I don't answer, he begins to pound on the door. I cover my ears with my hands and squeeze my eyes shut.

You're acting like a child, I tell myself. That only makes me cry more hot tears.

Abruptly, the numbing torrent of water stops and a large towel falls over my shoulders. Gentle hands lift me from the floor of the shower.

Embarrassed, I try to wiggle out of Pravat's grip. "I-I'm…I-I'm…" But my teeth chatter so much I can't get the words out. I retch again, and Pravat quickly positions my head over the toilet. It's all dry heaves, though.

After closing the lid, Pravat sits on it and peels off my shirt before vigorously rubbing my hair, chest, and arms with the towel. Then he strips off my pajama pants and dries my lower body while I stare miserably down at him, eyes blurry from crying.

IN LOVE

After leading me back to bed, he joins me under the blankets. Soothed by the warmth and skin-to-skin contact, I eventually calm down.

"I'm sorry," I mumble into the pillow.

"You have nothing to be sorry for," Pravat murmurs next to my ear.

I swallow. I have to know. "What did she say to you?"

"After I found out who it was on the phone, I didn't let her say anything. I hung up."

Digesting that, I turn and nestle into his arms.

"Thank you."

"You don't have to thank me," Pravat says against my hair.

"Yes, I do. Thank you for not listening to her. For believing me. She's trying to tell everyone I'm making it all up."

Pravat gently strokes my back. "Of course she is. She's guilty."

Squeezing my eyes shut, I whisper, "They believe her."

"Your father and sister stand behind you, and so do I. The rest probably don't know what to believe. They're still in shock."

Burrowing my face into his chest, I close my eyes.

"I wish I could go back and change things somehow. I wish that it never happened at all."

"It would save you a lot of pain, but your life would also be different. You'd be different."

I laugh mirthlessly. "Yeah, I wouldn't be such a wreck."

He kisses my head. "You wouldn't be as understanding, thoughtful, and intuitive."

Pulling back, I look at him. "Do you really see me that way? Understanding and thoughtful? Don't you know that everyone considers me cold and unyielding? Even the girls I've dated."

Continuing to stroke my back, Pravat says, "You've never been that way with me."

"You make it easy," I say, resting my head on his chest again.

"Your aunt took away your ability to trust. It's understandable. But inside, you're a sensitive, empathetic person because of what you've been through, and I happen to care about that person very much."

I've only ever thought about the negative ways in which I've changed, never imagining there could be anything positive.

As I lie there thinking about this, the room fills with Pravat's gentle snores, and I can't help but smile.

CHAPTER SIX:

Pravat

♥

Judging from the position of the sun, it must be close to nine a.m. Rama really scared me before, his raised voice waking me from a deep slumber. Then he locked himself in the bathroom. When I heard him retching and sobbing on the other side of the door, I wanted nothing more than to get to him and wrap him in my arms. But first I picked up his phone from the floor and spoke to the person on the other end. I didn't lie to Rama—as soon as his aunt identified herself, I told her I had nothing to say and hung up.

I had to break the lock on the door to get to Rama. I found him in the bathtub, still in his pajamas, shivering under ice-cold water, his face the picture of heartbreaking misery.

Against my chest, Rama groans. "What time is it? Did I fall asleep? We have to be at the studio."

Lifting my head, I peer over him at the clock on the bedside table to see I was correct about the time. "We're okay for a few more minutes."

Taking his face between my hands, I kiss him softly. I mean it as a comforting good morning, but he responds enthusiastically, parting his lips and arching his body against mine. Immediately, my cock fills inside my shorts. More than anything, I want to make him mine. But sex isn't what Rama needs from me right now. Pulling away, I kiss his nose.

"Maybe you should tell your father about the phone call. Let him deal with your aunt."

Rama stares at me a moment, and I can almost see him warring with himself. He wants to be distracted. I get that. But now is not the time. Finally, he nods, his hand skimming my side and leaving a trail of goosebumps. Pressing a kiss to my collarbone before sitting up, he seems to be reminding me what I'm missing. *Believe me, I know.*

"Come on," he says. "P'Tida will have our heads if we delay filming."

Rama's so flushed and beautiful, I nearly change my mind, but he throws back the covers and gets out of bed. His body is beautiful—all muscle and sinew and golden skin, and when he turns away from me, his round ass taunts me as he slips into his clothes.

Dragging my eyes away, I roll onto my stomach and blank out my mind until my erection subsides and I'm able to join him to brush my teeth.

· ♥ · ♥ · ♥ · ♥ · ♥ ·

As soon as we enter the studio, we're hustled to hair and makeup. I blush crimson when the woman tuts at the love bite on my collarbone before covering it with concealer.

Today we're filming several scenes outdoors, which always brings a new set of issues. The weather is clear and only slightly breezy, thank goodness, but a crowd has already gathered on the other side of the cordoned area of the street. When they spot us, the group seems to grow in number as they excitedly try to get closer but are held back by security.

The scene calls for Rama and me to walk side-by-side down the busy street while delivering our lines. I take a last look at my script as one of the crew fiddles with the sash at the front of Rama's shirt.

The moment Maha calls for action, a blaring alarm goes off somewhere close-by and lasts so long he has to send a runner to find the source.

Alarm finally silenced, we begin again only to have to stop moments later when Rama's sleeve gets caught on the edge of a post and rips. While waiting for one of the crew to fetch him a new shirt, Rama and I crouch on the pavement, flipping our empty water bottles in a competition to see who can land theirs upright. I can see people in the crowd taking pictures, and, wanting to touch him under the guise of fanservice, I reach out and push Rama's hair out of his eyes.

When the crew member returns with Rama's shirt, we straighten up. Rama strips off his ripped one, and the fans go wild, then boo when I step between them and the peep show.

A hand touches my arm, and I turn to find Lin.

"P'Tida sent me over to make sure I get in some of the videos," she says. At this rate, filming one short outdoor scene is going to take us all day.

When Rama's ready, we begin again, only to have the scene spoiled by a stray dog running between us. It might be comical if the holdup wasn't eating up precious time and the production company's money. After attempt number six, Maha calls for a break.

"This is a fiasco," Rama murmurs to me as one of the makeup people touches up his face with powder. I nod, having thought the same thing when the wind suddenly picked up and blew a stray paper into my face during the last take. It's as though fate doesn't want us to film this scene today.

A headache has taken up in the back of my skull, and I ask for some pain reliever.

"I'll get it," Lin says and heads to the first-aid station.

"Your hands are blackened from that newspaper," she tells me when she returns. As soon as I swallow the pill, she begins wiping my fingers with a wet wipe.

The following day, videos of this moment are posted on all the bl fan sites. Somehow, the simple gesture has been turned into a romantic interlude that have fans talking.

Boyzluvxx: I knew Pravat wasn't gay.

BLboy2004: Look at Rama's face! He's so hurt! My poor baby!!!

PravamaStan1: Omg!

Sunmaiden13: Wait. I'm confused. I thought Pravat was gay?

Pravma4evr@Sunmaiden13: He is. The woman is just helping him. She's probably giving him pain reliever or something.

BLboy2004: He has hands. Why is she wiping them for him?

Pravma4evr@BLboy2004: You've got a point there.

Boyzluvxx: Don't feed into rumors. His sexuality has never been confirmed.

BTSfanluvsJK: Maybe he's bi.

chimmysgirl@BTSfanluvsJK: It's none of our business. Stop speculating.

> **HazyDazy16104**: Is this the same girl from the other photos? She looks like she's in love with him.
>
> **Chanbaek_sees@HazyDazy16104**: Who wouldn't be? Look at those eyes! They look like they can see into my soul!
>
> **Animelvrbb**: Look at those…everything! :D
>
> **Taesgrl2003@HazyDazy16104**: Def the same girl.
>
> **JKtae4evr16104**: Do you think they're dating?
>
> **Pravma4evr**: Jesus, she's wiping his hands. Everyone needs to chill.

I study Rama's face in the video. Does he really look hurt? The fans make a big deal about everything, and, as Tida intended, many seem to think Lin and I are an item. Suddenly gloomy, I think, *Why can't I be up front about who I'm really attracted to, especially now that I have someone in my life I really want to be close to?*

I don't know why I'm torturing myself about it. Caught up in a money game, I don't have any choice but to go along.

CHAPTER SEVEN: Rama

♥

"Suzanne called me this morning to go over the guest list for Pete's wedding," my father tells me over breakfast one morning.

Suzanne is Pete's mother. His father, Pavel, is my father's oldest brother. Both have recently moved back to Thailand after years living in the United States.

This is my opening to tell my father about Pete's doubts concerning Aunt Sunnee, but if I do that, it might cause more bad feelings in the family. For the same reason, I haven't told him about Aunt Sunnee's call.

"Is it a large list?" I ask.

"No, maybe sixty people. It's going to take place outdoors, which I think is a good thing as long as the weather's not too hot. I assume you're going to be Pete's best man?"

I concentrate on the apple I'm peeling so I don't have to look at my father. "I don't think so. Pete hasn't asked me."

My father looks up from scrolling through his phone. "He hasn't?"

"No. He has a lot of friends. I wasn't counting on his asking me," I lie, watching the apple peel form a perfect coil on the cutting board.

Chinda walks into the kitchen, grabs a banana, and walks back out.

"What's up with your sister lately?" Pah asks, frowning as he looks at his watch. He's dressed in the clothes he wore for a run and probably thinks he'd better hurry and shower so he can get to the office, even though it's a Saturday.

"She's probably busy with classes."

"How's filming going?" Pah asks. Initially unhappy with my choice of career, he's been more supportive since my *episode* while in America. I know I should just enjoy it, but it doesn't mean the same when it comes from worry that I'll have another breakdown.

"It's going well. I have today and tomorrow off while they're filming the rest of the story for the secondary characters."

"Those are the two you say fight all the time? Mint and…"

"Two, yes. I'm sure the crew will be glad to be done working with them. Their constant bickering gets old."

"But you get along well with your costar, right? How is it I haven't met him yet? You should invite him to dinner tonight."

I almost choke on the slice of apple I just put into my mouth. My father wants to meet Pravat?

"Go on, Rama. Invite him. I don't bite." He grins at me.

Wiping my hands on a napkin, I ask myself what I'm so worried about. It isn't as though Pah knows about the nature of my relationship with Pravat. I send him a text, and while waiting for his answer, scroll through my phone. TikTok is full of posts of Pravat and Lin. Several of the pictures are new. One in particular catches my eye: Pravat and Lin walking out of a movie theater, holding hands. I stare at it a long time, blinking only when a text notification vibrates my phone.

"He can come," I tell my father.

"Great. Tell him to come around six. I'll have something catered." I type out the message, and Pah goes to his room to dress, leaving me with conflicting feelings. I'm jealous, there's no doubt about that. I don't like seeing Pravat with Lin. I don't like them holding hands. And I don't like the dozens of comments saying what a cute couple they make. But I do like the positive feedback for Pravat for a change. He deserves it. I can't imagine how he's felt since Preed accused him of trying to seduce him into bed. That was over two years ago. And who has Pravat had to lean on? Only his friends at school. He no longer has any family.

A part of me wants so much to be able to go out with Pravat and hold hands like that. But I have to be honest with myself and admit another part of me shies away from letting the world know I'm interested in a man. I hate myself for those feelings.

I throw my apple peel and core into the trash before heading outside to sit by the pool. Chinda's already out there on one of the lawn chairs, half her face hidden behind a large pair of sunglasses.

"Pravat's coming to dinner," I tell her, stripping off my shirt. I lower myself into the pool.

"He is? How did that happen?"

"Pah asked me to invite him." I push off the side and swim the length a dozen times before stopping and pulling myself out of the water to sit on the edge.

"Aren't you afraid Pah will realize what's up between you two?" Chinda picks up the conversation again.

I dry off with the towel before rising to sit on the lounge chair beside hers. Finally, I answer. "What do you mean?"

Chinda rolls her eyes. "Someone only has to be in the same room with you two to realize you guys are together."

"Don't be ridiculous," I say.

"Come off it, Rama. What, are you worried I'll spread it all over the fan sites? Give me some credit."

I trust her. And maybe this is the olive branch I need to extend to get us on the right track again. "Okay, so maybe we're kind of together."

Chinda's squeal nearly breaks my eardrums. "I knew it!"

I point at her. "But you have to keep it to yourself! I'm serious. This could hurt Pravat's career."

"I know, I know. When did you first realize you liked him?"

I sigh. "Can we please have this conversation some other time?" I look at her. "What's been up with you lately? You've been acting weird around me."

"What? I haven't been acting weird."

"Tell me the truth. Do you think I made up all that about Aunt Sunnee?"

"No!" Chinda exclaims so vehemently I believe her.

Still, I ask, "Are you sure about that?"

"Of course, stupid." She looks down at her hands. "I heard you on the phone with Alex. Pete doesn't believe you?"

"No, he doesn't."

"Are you sure? Maybe—"

"I could tell he didn't when I told him about it. He kept asking me if I was sure I was remembering correctly. He said the Aunt Sunnee he knows would never do such a thing, and that she often sat on his bed and talked to him at night when he was that age. He asked me if that could be what she'd done and I'd somehow misconstrued it." I let out a mirthless laugh. "As if I could mistake a late-night talk for sexual assault."

"So, Aunt Sunnee...touched you?"

I look away. "Suffice it to say there is no way I could have mistaken one for the other. And it happened more than once." I clench my fists. "How could Pete think I'd lie about something like that?"

"I haven't known what to say about it to you. And after I saw how angry you got with Alex, I was afraid to bring it up. Sorry if I was acting weird."

"It's okay. I know it's all really awkward."

"It's probably easier for me to accept than it is for Pete, though. I hardly know Aunt Sunnee. She hasn't been around much the last several years."

After I dry off, I go inside and shower, wanting to be ready when Pravat arrives. I wonder if I can get him alone for a minute. One of his hugs would go a long way in making me feel better.

CHAPTER EIGHT: Pravat

Rama's family estate with its gated property, modern house, swimming pool, and tennis court is located just outside Bangkok's city limits. Looking at it, I feel every inch of my lower-income, orphan status.

After ringing the front doorbell, I wait on the porch, looking at the manicured lawn. I expect to see a servant when the door opens, but it's Rama's younger sister. She gives me a shy smile and the wai when she sees me.

"P'Pravat, come in. My brother's out back. I hope you're in the mood for some American BBQ. Pah was going to have everything catered, but then he brought home pork ribs. Don't worry, I've made some fish balls and rice in case you don't want the pork."

"Anything's fine, Nong," I say, stepping into the air-conditioned house that smells of polished wood.

A tall older man dressed in casual slacks and a short-sleeved collared shirt strides into the room. I can immediately tell he's Rama's father because they look quite a bit alike, although Rama's features are softer and, well, *prettier*.

"You must be Pravat," he says. "I'm Korn Sathianthai."

"Sawasdee khrap," I say, giving him the wai, and we chat a moment about the weather before he sends me out the sliding glass doors to see how Rama's coming along with the pork. The back patio is shaded by a long awning, and Rama stands just beyond it in front of a large charcoal grill. This is truly American barbecue with the meat directly on the grill and no boil of vegetables. When Rama sees me, a smile lights up his face.

Coming to stand close to him, I look over his shoulder. It's the sweet smell of his skin and not the tang of the meat I'm admiring.

"That smells delicious."

Turning the ribs with a pair of tongs, Rama says, "I'm glad you could come."

"I was a little surprised at the invitation," I say.

"It was Pah's idea. I think he just thought it was about time he met you. Is he the one who let you in?"

"No, Chinda let me in. But I met him. He told me to come out here."

Setting down the tongs, Rama turns to look at me, his expression troubled. "I want to tell him about, well, our true relationship. I just don't know how."

Heart leaping at his words, I smile. "This is new for you. Maybe you should allow yourself to get used to it before you try to explain it to anyone else. Just the fact that you want to tell him is enough for me."

Rama doesn't look convinced. Peering behind me, he surprises me by pressing a quick kiss to my mouth.

"I've been wanting to do that for days," he says with a sigh when our lips part.

We haven't been alone much since Rama last stayed with me at my apartment. Our long work schedule the past couple of weeks has made it necessary for us to sleep at the studio where even a moment's privacy is difficult to come by.

I smile at him. "Me, too."

When we enter the house with the plate of cooked ribs, Chinda has just finished setting the large dining room table. The three of us carry the rest of the food in from the kitchen.

"Pravat, tell me about yourself. Are you from Bangkok?" Korn asks when we're seated.

"Yes, Uncle," I say, hoping I don't sound as nervous as I am. I'm not about to tell him I'm from one of the poorest areas of the city.

"Pravat's father died when he was young. He helped his mother bring up his siblings," Rama explains to his father.

"You sound like a dutiful son," his father says. "I'm sure your mother is very proud. Does she live near you?"

"My mother and siblings passed away a few years ago in a fire," I say. It's something I've had to repeat many times, and I've learned not to let the words sink in deeply enough to affect me.

Rama's father frowns. "I'm sorry." He changes the subject, and the rest of the meal is accompanied by light conversation.

Looking at Korn Sathianthai, I can see why Rama was afraid to open up to him about the past. He's an imposing man, tall and broad with the same stern expression often seen on his son's face, although never directed at me. Rama's narrower build, pretty features, and graceful movements must have come from his mother. What would the man think if he knew his son was involved with someone like me? Not only a man, but someone without family or a good name? Benjawan wasn't even my real last name, it was my godfather's—another person close to me who passed on.

Later, when the meal is finished and Rama and I sit by the swimming pool watching the moon rising above the distant tree line, Rama says, "I could never have done this without you."

Looking at him, I raise a brow. "Done what? Cooked the ribs?" I tease.

He pokes my arm. "No. The series. Telling my dad. Pretty much everything I've done this past year and a half to move myself forward."

"Of course you could have done it. You took the first step to audition. I didn't win you that part. And you told your father about your aunt. All I did was encourage you."

"No one's ever encouraged me before."

I squeeze his hand. "You're an amazing person, Rama Sathianthai. Don't let anyone tell you otherwise."

Hearing the sliding glass door open, I drop his hand and lean my head back on the cushioned chair.

"Don't stop on my account," Chinda says, walking to the edge of the pool. She's changed into a bathing suit.

I look at Rama in surprise. His sister knows about us?

"She's incorrigible," Rama says. "I had to confirm it or she'd never leave me alone."

"That's right," Chinda says with a grin. "Don't worry, your secret's safe with me. But you'd better be careful. What if I'd been Pah?"

"How do you think he'd react if he found out?" Rama asks.

Chinda's quiet a moment. "I'm not sure. Okay, I think. But it would be better if you told him instead of his walking in on the two of you. Are you two going to swim?" She dips her toe in the water.

"Do you want to?" Rama asks me. "I have some trunks you can wear."

"I think I'll pass," I say. "But don't let that stop you from getting in."

Rama shrugs. "I can swim anytime." He cocks his head. "What did you do today?"

"I saw that new action movie that just came out."

When Rama doesn't reply, I realize he's probably seen the pictures of me and Lin online.

"P'Tida called me last night and told me she'd gotten tickets for me and Lin."

"Was it any good?" His eyes are trained on Chinda's butterfly strokes across the pool.

"Pretty much like every other action film I've seen. A lot of blowing things up. Does it bother you that I'm having to do this?"

Turning to look at me, Rama frowns. "I—" he stops and sighs heavily. "Yes."

I open my mouth to tell him Lin means nothing to me and that I'm gay anyway and could never be attracted to her, but he interrupts.

"I'm jealous that it can't be me. That we can't go to the movie and hold hands that way. That we can't kiss in public." His voice rises slightly. "That I'm too damned chicken to tell my own father about us."

In the moonlight, his eyes shine like black marbles. I lower my gaze to his lush lips, longing to kiss them. "After the series—"

"After the series there'll be another series. And another. And another," Rama says bitterly.

"What are you saying?" Fear, as sudden as the southerly breeze that's built up, coils in my gut.

Chinda stops swimming and climbs out of the pool. As she's drying off with the towel, she must notice the tension between us because she mumbles something about a test she needs to study for and hurries inside the house.

"Rama," I say, trying to keep my voice level when I feel like my world is about to crash down around me. "If this is too much for you..." I leave off, unable to finish the sentence. *What? I'm not going to let him break up with me.*

Turning to face me, Rama gives me a stern look, but I can see the vulnerability under it.

"I just said how much I want to be with you. Why would you take that as wanting to break things off?"

"Why? You've found yourself suddenly attracted to a man, and now you have to deal with the subterfuge, the long hours, the impossibility of being alone other than to sleep." I clench my fists. "Anyone would choose an easier route than this."

In one graceful move, Rama leaves his chair and straddles my lap, placing his hands on my face.

"I'm never leaving you." His lips descend on mine, strong and sure.

All coherent thought leaving my head, my hands lose their grip on the chair and move to his waist, slender and firm beneath my palms. My fingers itch to slide under the soft cotton of his shirt to feel the smooth skin beneath.

It takes me a moment to come to my senses and push him back. He looks so sexy—hair disheveled from the breeze and lips pink and swollen from our kiss—it's all I can do not to tug him back down and do all the things I've dreamed of doing for months. But we're in his backyard, where his father only has to look out a window to see us.

As though he's suddenly remembered, Rama's eyes fly to the sliding glass doors behind me. When he stiffens in my lap, I know without having to ask what he sees.

"Up," I say, patting his leg. "Rama, get up."

He obeys. I look over my shoulder. Behind the glass, Rama's father stands, face pale with obvious shock.

Swallowing, I turn back to Rama, expecting to see fear and shame on his face. I'm surprised when I instead see fierce determination. Before I can speak, he reaches between us and grasps my hand, lacing our fingers together.

"No matter what," he says calmly, "I'm going back with you to your place tonight."

Then he steps toward the house.

CHAPTER NINE: Rama

♥

When I've imagined telling my father about my relationship with Pravat, the worst part is always in finding the words and seeing the expression on Pah's face after I say them.

The former is taken away from me when Pah catches us kissing on the back patio. It's my fault. I'm the one who climbed onto Pravat's lap and fused our mouths together in a desperate move to make him understand my feelings. Seeing him sitting there, trying to do what he undoubtedly thought was the right thing and let me go, broke me. I can't lose him, and that's all there is to it. So, maybe it's for the best that Pah saw us. I'm sure I'll be able to see that later, but for now I'm nervous.

Pah's expression is full of shock, but I don't see any anger.

When I slide open the door to the house, Pah takes a step back.

"I'm sorry I didn't tell you," I say. Hopefully I haven't misjudged his reaction and won't be sent to the floor by his fist. He's never hit me, but there's always a first time. "I've been trying to figure out how to do it. I'm also sorry for that open display in your home, Pah."

IN LOVE

Beside me, Pravat squeezes my hand reassuringly. Now that I stand before my father, I'm shaking. What a disappointment I must be to him—first in revealing myself to be damaged from his sister's abuse, then to reveal I'm in love with a man.

"I don't understand," my father says. "Weren't you rehearsing?"

Mouth parting in surprise, I glance at Pravat, whose eyes clearly convey this is my chance to get out of this.

I shake my head.

"No, Pah. I won't lie to you. We have to lie to everyone else."

"I see." My father turns and walks to the living room, and Pravat and I follow.

My father sits on the large chair by the fireplace and motions us to the couch.

"Explain," he says, voice even.

"I fell in love with Pravat," I say. When I hear Pravat's indrawn breath, I realize neither of us have ever put our feelings into words. I clasp his hand hard. "I didn't expect it, but that's what happened, Pah."

My father's eyes go to Pravat. "Are you in love with my son?"

"Don't—" I begin, but Pravat cuts me off.

"Yes."

"Your roles may be confusing you," Pah says.

I swallow. This has occurred to me. But from the get-go, Pravat broke through my walls, and I responded to him like I never have with anyone else. Isn't that an indication of the feelings I have for him?

"No," I say. "That's not it."

"Rama, this is your first acting role," Pah says matter-of-factly. "How could you know it isn't going to be like this every time?"

"I acted in two plays when I stayed with Pete and Alex the first time. My character had a love interest in one, and I didn't think I was in love with her."

"But the bl industry's different. You've explained about the skinship. I've seen the videos of fanmeetings and talk shows."

I'm momentarily struck dumb. My father has watched the videos?

"It isn't the same," Pravat says. "I've done this several times, and I never had this type of feeling. There's always a distinct divide when the attention is off."

"But Rama is new to it. He's never considered being with a man before and discovering an attraction could easily be construed into something more."

Letting go of Pravat's hand, I stand abruptly.

"Don't try to plant doubts in my mind," I say angrily.

"Rama," Pah says. "Sit."

Stiffly, I obey.

"You have no right to dissect my feelings," I say tightly.

"I'm only trying to suggest to you what could be happening. You need to take things slowly," Pah says. "Don't be impulsive."

"Have I ever been impulsive?" I ask rigidly.

"You have, yes. You used to be quite impetuous."

Before what happened.

The words hang in the air.

"I've grown up," I say, adding bitterly, "Maybe too quickly."

Studying me a moment, my father asks, "So, you think you're gay? Or bisexual?"

Frowning, I say, "I—no. I don't have this attraction to anyone but Pravat."

Pah nods, as though he's confirmed something.

Annoyed, I burst out, "Do you accept my relationship, or do I need to pack up and leave?"

I feel Pravat stiffen beside me. I don't blame him—I've shocked even myself.

My father's lips firm. "If you're asking if I'm disowning you, the answer is no. I thought we'd made some headway in our relationship the past several months. Was I wrong?"

Like a stopper has been pulled, the anger flows out of me.

"I'm sorry. We have. I'm just feeling defensive."

"Did you expect me to be angry?"

"I wasn't sure how you would react. I know this must be a let-down for you," I mutter, eyes on my lap.

"Don't assume how I feel," Pay says sharply. "Haven't you just reprimanded me for doing the same to you?"

I hang my head lower. "I'm sorry, Pah."

A moment ticks by in silence before my father gets to his feet.

"You're a grown man, Rama," he says. "You're capable of making your own decisions. I only suggest that you keep your eyes wide open while you do."

When Pah walks away, Pravat rests his hand on my thigh.

"Are you all right?"

Taking a deep breath and letting it out, I nod. So many conflicting feelings are churning in me, I don't know what to say or do.

"Let's go to your place," I finally say.

Nodding, Pravat stands.

Twenty minutes later, we're unlocking the door to his apartment. I'm nervous, and I don't know why. I've spent many nights here, but after my proclamation to my father, this one feels different.

"Relax," Pravat says. I'm embarrassed he saw through me so easily.

Getting a couple of beers from the refrigerator, he sits beside me on the couch.

"I'm sorry," he says after a moment.

I look at him incredulously. "About what? I'm the one who crawled on top of you out there where my father could so easily see us." I sigh. "Maybe I wanted him to."

"Your father didn't react too badly," Pravat says.

"No. But he doubts us."

"He just wants you to be careful."

Thinking about that kiss out on the patio, I set my beer on the table. When I do the same with his bottle, Pravat looks at me questioningly. I move closer.

Although our series occasionally pushes the relatively chaste boys' love envelope, most of the kisses Pravat and I have shared on-screen have happened with several careful inches between us—much less than some actors put between themselves and their costar, but still there. It doesn't make any sense, but I realized quickly when I started acting in this genre that it isn't popular for its realism. Now, with none of that space between us, I let out a sigh as I press Pravat backward into the couch and slot my lips over his.

How can I be so attracted to another man? I wonder as everything lights up within me at the intimate contact. He's the only man who's ever made me feel off balance when he comes near me, his every touch leaving me wanting more.

When he nibbles on my lower lip, I open my mouth to him, and t wet slide of his tongue against mine sends a shiver down my back. I sink farther into him.

"Rama." The way he says my name so hoarsely makes me crazy, and I kiss him with more fervor.

"Whoa, slow down." Pravat adjusts us so we're lying on our sides, face-to-face. "We've got plenty of time."

I've lost all control, something that's never happened to me before when it came to sex. I can't think straight. "I need you," I manage to say before collapsing, my face finding the juncture of his neck and shoulder.

"I need you, too," Pravat says softly, combing his fingers through my hair. When I withdraw to look at him, he kisses me. I think it's meant to be a light, soft kiss, but it quickly turns into something fiery and desperate that has us grappling with each other's clothing, throwing it piece by piece onto the floor until we're both down to our boxer briefs.

Clasping my face in his hands, Pravat pulls our lips apart. I stare at his messy hair and wild eyes.

"What...what do you want to do?" he asks. Licking his lips, he adds, "I mean, we don't have to go any further than this."

"Everything," I say. "But you're going to have to show me."

CHAPTER TEN:
Pravat

♥

Rama's words are like matches to straw, immediately setting me aflame. Sitting up, I tug him to his feet and over to the bed.

With the last vestiges of my control, I say, "Please tell me if I do anything you don't like."

Rama nods, and I kiss him. Deeply, possessively, the way I've wanted to for so long but have always held myself back because I didn't want to scare him. And he melts beneath me, lips drinking from mine.

Rama groans as I bite and lick at the tempting column of his neck. "Pravat, please."

My resolve to take this slowly cracks. I have some experience, but not a lot. I don't want to hurt him or do anything that might bring back memories of the trauma he suffered.

"Are you...will this..." I can't seem to put the question into words, and my hesitation threatens to throw ash on the flames. Closing my eyes, I take a deep breath, forcing the words from my lips. "Will any of this remind you of what happened...years ago?"

When I open my eyes, Rama's are wet.

"I'm sorry," I rush to say. "I shouldn't have mentioned it." Silently cursing myself, I start to back off from where I have him pinned on the bed, thinking I've ruined everything before it's begun.

Rama's fingers tighten on my arms, holding me still. "No. Nothing you do reminds me of that. Thank you for asking."

I pause, staring down at him, and he takes that moment to surge upward, toppling me to my back on the mattress and rolling to loom over me. The way his gaze slowly roams down my body makes my already stiff cock twitch painfully.

Rama kisses me, and I clutch the firm muscles of his back, small moans escaping my mouth only to immediately be eaten by his questioning lips.

When he lowers his body onto mine and our groins align, I push upward, creating glorious friction, stoking the flame and taking us higher and higher until we stop kissing altogether and simply pant into the other's mouth, completely focused on the rhythmic motions of our hips.

"Pravat...Pravat..." Rama chants, each repetition getting a little louder and a little more broken until he's nearly sobbing my name as he grinds against me, both of our cocks rigid inside our shorts.

I want so much to get rid of that last layer of clothing between us, but I'm afraid to take things too far too fast. It isn't only Rama's past trauma I have to worry about—this is also his first time with a man, and I don't want to freak him out.

Then again, the desperate way Rama grinds against me, sending intense ripples of pleasure from my groin to the top of my head and tips of my toes tells me he might be more on board with this than I thought. Already, I'm getting closer and closer to the edge. Rama's breath falls hot on my neck, and our hearts pound together through our sweat-slick skin as we strain together. So close...*so close*.

Latching my hands onto his ass, I squeeze hard, pushing against him until I shatter. The last thing I see before closing my eyes to the wave of euphoria is Rama's pleasure-clouded gaze. As I float on my high, I feel him jolt against me, and the small whimpers he makes send another charge of pleasure through me.

I come back to myself with Rama's full weight on top of me, our hearts beating fast and furious against each other. Pressing a kiss to his shoulder, I taste the salt of his sweat. He shivers.

"Okay?" I ask breathlessly. I want to laugh. To shout. To do something to mark this moment.

Rama's chuckle reverberates through me. "More than," he says, rolling off me.

Looking down at the damp spot at the front of my boxers, I vaguely think of getting up and cleaning us off, but my body is boneless.

"Fuck, that was good," Rama says with a tired sigh.

Summoning up all my energy, I roll to my side to look at him. His expression is lax, eyes languidly drooping. Suddenly, he frowns. "It was, wasn't it?" he asks uncertainly.

I smile. "It definitely was." I push myself up. "I'll be right back."

In the bathroom, I soak a cloth with warm water and clean myself up before returning to him. I change my shorts while he takes care of himself, then toss a pair of clean ones onto the bed for him to change into.

"So, now I know what sex with a man is like," Rama says.

"There's more to it than that," I say, joining him on the bed.

The tips of his ears turn red. "Oh, well, yeah. Of course."

I've had exactly one boyfriend before Rama. I met Sud in university my freshman year. Our relationship was an on and off thing, the last part extending long enough for us to get to the point where we were comfortable in our sex life, and we started experimenting a little. But then I started my acting career, and Sud couldn't handle the jealousy.

I resisted looking for another relationship for a long time after we broke up. I definitely wasn't looking for one when I met Rama, after all the negative publicity about my sexuality Preed had stirred up, but something about him tugged at my heart.

"Hey," Rama says. I look from where I'd been staring out the window at the river. He's rumpled and looks incredibly inviting lying in my bed, and when he beckons to me, I go to him, slipping beneath the covers and wrapping my arms around him. He sighs as he rests his cheek on my chest.

"I was probably really awkward," he says. "I'll get better with practice."

My heart stutters, both at his self-doubt and the fact that he's already talking about doing more with me.

"You were great. I'm the one who was awkward. It's been a while for me."

"I figured you've been with a lot of guys." Rama sounds surprised.

"Why?" I ask.

"Because you're hot."

I huff a laugh. "I've only had one relationship."

"The guy who got jealous of your work?" he asks.

"Yeah. Sud. Looking back, I can see we weren't very good together. It was mostly convenience. You've only ever been with women, right?" I ask, even though I know already.

"Yeah."

"Was what we just did...disappointing?"

"No, not at all. I wasn't sure what to expect, to be honest. I've never been close emotionally to the women I've dated. That seems to make a difference. And I've never thought of just grinding against someone like that to get off. It was a lot hotter than I would have guessed."

I stroke his back. Rama's breathing becomes even and heavy, but I don't sleep for a long time, preferring to enjoy having him in my arms for as long as I can.

CHAPTER ELEVEN: Rama

I'm not sure why I feel so embarrassed. I've had sex with a dozen women and have never blushed like a kid caught with porn the way I do every time Pravat looks at me these days.

Even more ridiculous, it's been over a week since we—I feel my cheeks heat at the thought—fooled around. *Fooled around? How old am I?* Had sex. We had sex that night.

Maybe if I allowed myself to think about it, to analyze it, I'd understand the difference. One change is definitely that I have feelings for Pravat, whereas I never have for any of the women I've been with. I was meeting a physical need with them and nothing else. Looking back, feeling the way I do now, I kind of hate myself for it. How awful would it feel for Pravat to treat me with the disregard that I treated those girls with? I'm ashamed.

Another difference is the off-balance, trembling feeling I've been left went since we did what we did. Every look, every touch—no matter how innocuous—from him is a hot lick of flame, and it's invariably followed by this extreme shyness that I'm feeling now.

And Pravat, the fucker, always gives me that knowing smile, like he knows exactly what I'm thinking and exactly how my body's reacting to him.

He's doing it right now, and I have to look away, cheeks hot.

Shouldn't I be annoyed? Disgusted with myself over my reaction to him? I've always prided myself on my independence, but it seems Pravat can't do anything that provokes a negative reaction out of me. Is this what love is?

"Rama."

I jump at the voice calling my name. Turning, I find Mint standing too close. Where did he come from? Since when can people enter my personal space without my realizing it? I really am a goner for Pravat. I take a step back, glancing to where Pravat's attention has been diverted from me to Maha and the script he's holding.

"What?" I answer Mint.

"I said your name three times," he says. "What in the world were you thinking about?"

"Dinner," I say easily. *Well, I probably was drooling.* "What can I do for you?"

"I want to run through the scene with you again."

I'm barely able to hold in my groan. The scene he's referring to is one where Mint's character comes onto mine. I've been dreading it since the day I first read it. We've run through our lines several times, but Mint's a fucking perfectionist.

"What exactly is it you're worried about?" I ask. "Is it the kiss?"

Mint makes a face, the homophobic asshole. Maybe he'll get lucky and hit it big soon, so he can move onto a genre less disgusting to him.

Grabbing me by the elbow, Mint leads me to a side room, shutting the door behind him.

I jerk my arm away. "What the hell?"

IN LOVE

Mint puffs out a breath. "Yes, it's the kiss," he says between clenched teeth.

I wait for an explanation. When none comes, I say, "Surely you don't want to practice *that*."

"Don't worry, I'm not any more eager than you are to lock lips. Although you do it easily enough with Pravat. And you know *he* enjoys it."

"What's that supposed to mean?" I ask, drawing myself up.

"You know exactly what it means. He's a fruit." When I start to say something, he holds up his hand. "Come on, you know it's true. I'm not saying he came onto Preed, necessarily. That guy's a prick and I don't believe a word that comes out of his mouth. But it's pretty obvious from the way Pravat's always looking at your ass that he wants a piece of it. That bullshit with Lin isn't fooling anybody."

"Shut up," I say coolly. I want to punch his stupid, arrogant face so badly I can taste it. "Just shut your fucking mouth." I start for the door.

"Where the hell are you going?" he calls after me. "We have a scene to rehearse!"

"We've rehearsed it enough, and I'm not practicing that kiss with you. If you aren't a good enough actor to do it, you need to find another job."

Opening the door, I walk back into the common room, Mint spluttering behind me. Pravat's eyes catch mine, and I give him a small smile even though I'm seething inside. *Fucking Mint.*

The scene goes well because, as much as I'd like to deny it, Mint *is* a good actor. The kiss amounts to Mint's character forcing himself on mine with a cold press of lips, while I try to shove him off. This is the first kiss I've experienced with a man other than Pravat, and I don't like it. Then Pravat's character enters, grabs Mint by the shoulder, and, swinging him around, punches him.

Fake punches him. But that isn't what happens. What Pravat does is a little too aggressive, a little too *real*, sending Mint flying into the wall. Maha calls for the scene to cut. Mint scrambles to his feet, holding his jaw, and charges, grabbing fists full of Pravat's shirt and pushing him backward into the cameraman, who barely manages to save his mounted piece of expensive equipment from crashing to the floor.

"Stop!" Maha yells, he and Nahn grabbing Mint's arms from behind.

"What the hell is going on here?" Maha demands.

"I didn't mean to actually hit him like that," Pravat says.

"Like hell you didn't!" Mint shouts.

Inserting his sturdy frame between them, Maha holds his hands out as though to keep each of them back, although Mint's the only one taking an aggressive stance at this point.

"I got carried away with the role," Pravat says. "I'm sorry I nicked you."

"*Nicked* me? You full-on punched me, you motherfucking *faggot*! You didn't like it that someone else had their lips on your man!"

Fury explodes in Pravat's eyes, and he surges forward. Grabbing him around his middle, I pull him back.

Nahm motions with his head to the security guards whose normally bored expressions have suddenly come to life. Springing into action, they drag a cursing Mint into the hall.

"Hey, what about him? What about *him*?" Mint shouts.

Pravat relaxes, and I let him go.

"I'm sorry," he says to Maha.

"There's no excuse for what he just said to you. Tida will handle him."

I can already hear our producer yelling in the corridor. When Maha leaves to join them, Pravat turns to me with a small smile.

"What was that?" I hiss. "And don't tell me you were just in character."

"I was a little bit, but I didn't try very hard to rein myself in."

"If I have to do that kiss over, I'm going to punch *you*." Relenting, I smile slightly. "I have to admit I enjoyed seeing him fly into the wall, though."

Pravat chuckles.

"He's trouble," I warn. "He doesn't like you, and now you've made him really mad."

Pravat shrugs. "It was worth it to connect my fist with that conceited face. Besides, guys like Mint are all bluster."

To my relief, rather than re-film the scene, Maha decides to keep the footage, warning everyone present that he'd better not find details of the moment on the gossip sites. After a touch-up by the makeup person, I search out Pravat and find him sitting on the couch with Lin practically on his lap, probably already trying to undo the damage. Rather than go to him as I'd first planned, I veer off and take a seat next to Two.

"I heard there was a tussle. Sorry I missed it," he says.

"Mint needs a fucking muzzle," I grumble.

Nodding his agreement, Two says, "I admit I'm pretty eager for this series to be released and the publicity to be over with. If I have to stand on stage and act like I like him much longer, I'm going to go crazy. P'Tida's starting to get annoyed with us, but I swear it's his fault. I'm really trying."

"Just shows what a good actor are," I say. "The fans think there's something between you."

Two makes a face. "As if. No amount of good looks can make up for that personality."

"Right?" We chuckle together.

After a moment, Two juts his chin toward Pravat and Lin. "What's going on with those two?"

Reluctantly, I glance their way. Lin's hand rests on Pravat's bicep, slender fingers squeezing the muscle as she smiles at him while he talks. I want to knock her hand off him.

Instead, I say lightly, although the words taste bitter in my mouth. "I guess they're dating."

"For real? I don't know. I don't see it."

"What do you mean?" I ask carefully. Pravat said that Tida gave strict instructions that no one but she, Pravat, and Lin were to know the relationship is a sham. Of course, she has no idea Pravat told me about it.

"He doesn't look at her like he's interested," Two says. "I've wondered if he really is gay. Not that I would out him," he assures me. "I don't care who he prefers to sleep with. You know him pretty well. What do you think?"

"I think it's real," I say. "Pravat's just a very private person."

Looking back at Pravat, who's laughing at something Lin said, Two nods. "Huh. Well, they make a cute couple."

"They certainly do," I agree, gut twisting.

CHAPTER TWELVE: Pravat

♥

The auditorium is packed with fans, the faces in the crowd blending into one another as I look out over them from the stage. Rama stands beside me, smiling and waving at the fans who hold up signs and make hearts symbols with their fingers.

This morning Tida called me, waking me from a vivid dream about Rama that I would have rather finished. The conversation was short and left me confused. Tida told me that, while she expected satisfactory fanservice today from me and Rama as usual, she didn't want us to overdo things. She was leaving it in my hands and trusted me to make the right decisions.

So, in consequence, I'm holding back, but I'm unsure how much to hold back. I haven't had the opportunity to tell Rama about Tida's call, but he's taking his cues from me, keeping a slight wall between us at all times while we remain affectionate in our interactions.

And I'm miserable.

Months ago, when Rama returned from America and confided in me about what his aunt had done to him when he was an adolescent, the already close relationship we'd developed while filming *My Doctor, My Love* strengthened exponentially. Our bond came at a time when I sorely needed it. It hasn't been long since I lost my family and coping with being completely alone in the world has been difficult, especially after Preed began his campaign to wreck my career. My best friend Kiet has been a rock for me, but how much can he take on and still live his own life? He has a girlfriend and his classes at university to worry about.

I could never have anticipated developing such strong feelings for Rama, especially in such a short amount of time. I definitely wouldn't have thought it possible when I first met him—he seemed so closed-off then, I couldn't imagine he would actually be able to *act*. But his audition not only impressed Tida and Maha, it left me reeling from a chemistry I didn't know was possible to feel with someone I just met.

This chemistry has been the secret of our success as well as the groundwork for a relationship we've been carefully building in hopes we could have something once this series is over. We would have to be careful, yes, but I really thought it was possible.

Now, I'm not so sure. If Tida is pulling us away from each other, it could only mean she's already thinking ahead to after the series has finished.

As pictures flash, Rama looks at me, eyes assessing behind the smile on his face. He knows something is up.

Leaning in, he places a quick peck to my cheek. The crowd goes nuts. I'll be blushing in all the photos. I can't help the smile that widens my mouth, and for a moment, we just stare at each other as the fans cheer.

The host asks Mint a question, and, reminding myself of the call from Tida, I turn my attention to him. He, too, has his arm draped around his co-star's waist, but from my vantage point I can see how loosely his hand rests on Two's belt, as well as the careful inches they keep between them. I've seen the postings on the fan sites about them, saying they have to be a real couple because they are just so adorable together. Those comments would be amusing if they didn't rankle so much. Why does the speculation only matter in my and Rama's case? *Is it because Tida knows it's true?*

She couldn't know.

But she could suspect.

Not necessarily, I tell myself. After all, it would be a little difficult to worry over Mint and Two's relationship when they're always at each other's throats when the cameras are off and no fans are present.

Between us, Rama's fingers link with mine, and he squeezes. At the left of the stage, I feel Tida's eyes on us, and I gently disentangle from his grip, using the excuse of digging into my pocket for a tissue to wipe at the sweat on my temple.

When the fan meeting is over, our bodyguards escort us from the auditorium, the cast nodding and smiling until we reach the privacy of the back hall.

"Holy shit, I think I'm deaf now," Mint says when we escape the din. "Somehow, I'm always shocked that young girls can scream that loud."

He's already put several feet of distance between himself and Two, although when Two stumbles on the stairs, he instantly shoots out an arm to catch him. *At least he's not a total pile of shit.* When I glance at Tida, she nods to me, letting me know she was satisfied. The emotional distance I'm feeling between myself and Rama worries me, but there isn't anything I can do about it at the moment. Not with so many people around us.

"Nice job, everybody," Tida says as we walk to our respective cars, security flanking us.

I repeat the words in my head: *Nice job*. None of the fanservice seemed like a job with Rama because none of it is faking for us. I glance at where he's folding himself into his silver Toyota Corolla and wonder what he's thinking.

My stomach contracts when he doesn't look my way before closing his car door and starting the engine. Turning toward my Miata, I keep my expression carefully blank and spend a minute checking the fan sites before I roll out of the parking lot.

Pravma fans seem happy enough, but some noticed the difference.

WuttheJenny: Anyone else think Pravat seemed off today?

Stargazer01@WuttheJenny: Glad I'm not the only one.

Gaybe2010: Our king seemed fine, though.

KPopdrop: Pravat was probably thinking about his girl. I'm sure Rama noticed.

The last statement was followed by a mixture of hearts and crying faces.

I'm exhausted. The second season coming so soon after the first has taken a lot out of me. A few more weeks and it will be over, but rather than looking forward to that, I'm dreading it. Rama and I planned to take a vacation together, but what if Tida somehow stops that from happening?

I drive by a nearby convenience store to pick up a few things before continuing to my building. When I step into my apartment, I let out a surprised shout when I find Rama there, sitting on my couch. I gave him a key, but I never expected to find him here waiting for me tonight.

He gets to his feet. "I hope it's okay I came by."

I set my package from the store onto the counter. "Of course it is. I just didn't expect it. You didn't even look at me when you left."

Rama bows his head. "Sorry. I didn't know how to act. P'Tida was watching us so closely, and now I feel like Mint's watching us, too."

I approach him, and Rama looks up at me, his dark eyes troubled.

"It's rough. But soon it will be over," I tell him even though I've been having similar worries.

"Will it? The constant scrutiny?"

"For a while, anyway." Reaching out, I touch his shoulder. "Are you all right?"

For a moment, Rama's handsome face transforms into the stoic mask he so often wears in front of other people, but it quickly vanishes.

"I'm fine. Are *you* all right?"

"Sure. I'm good. Just tired. I know you are, too."

I turn for the small kitchen. "I'm going to make a little something to eat. Hungry?"

"Starving," Rama says.

I begin chopping vegetables and heating oil in the large round skillet while Rama roams the apartment, studying my paintings.

"Don't peek at those in the corner," I tell him.

"I know, I know," Rama says. He knows I don't want him to see my gift to him until I'm finished.

When the food's ready, we sit down to eat.

Unable to ignore the worry in my gut any longer, I say, "You've seemed a little withdrawn lately."

Across the bar, Rama's eyes meet mine. "I have?"

I shrug. "You haven't slept over since the last time when we..." I let the sentence fall. We both know what I'm talking about.

"Actually, I've sensed a change in *you*."

"Really?" I ask, surprised. I didn't realize I've been acting any differently.

"Sometimes I've wondered if you might be..." Rama's voice tails off, the tips of his ears turning red.

"Might be what?" I prompt.

He shrugs. "I don't know. I'm just tired. Don't pay any attention to me."

Putting down my fork, I reach over and cover his hand with mine. "Nothing's changed for me," I say firmly.

"You seemed a little distant today," Rama says.

I let out a breath. So, he did notice. "P'Tida asked me to take things down a notch today."

"Why?"

"I don't know."

Rising from his stool, Rama comes around the bar and kneels at my feet, resting his head on my knee. My heart melts.

"My feelings are exactly the same as they've always been," he says. "No matter what anyone says or does."

Lightly stroking his thick hair, I can't speak for a moment for the emotion clogging my throat. Finally, I begin, "I was afraid—"

Jerking his head up, Rama looks at me intensely. "Afraid of what? You aren't some experiment to me, Pravat."

I nod. "Okay."

"You don't believe me?" he asks, dark brows forming a V over the straight line of his nose.

"I was just a little worried that what we did here that night might have freaked you out."

Getting to his feet, Rama crowds me on my stool until my back hits the wall. The focus of his eyes shifting between mine and the frown still on his face, he says. "I enjoyed what we did. I-I've wanted to do it again."

"But I feel like you've been avoiding me."

IN LOVE

Letting out a harsh sigh, Rama backs up slightly, looking away.

"Rama. What is it?"

"Sometimes I think you aren't pretending when you're with Lin," he mumbles.

"What? Why would you say that?" I tug his hand so he stands between my parted knees. "Rama."

Reluctantly, he meets my gaze. "I—maybe I'm seeing things that aren't there."

"Maybe?" My lips curl into a smile. "Try *definitely*. I'm only attracted to men. That's not something that can suddenly change."

"I've always been attracted to women but suddenly I find myself attracted to you," he points out.

Ah. Tugging him closer, I rest my head on his chest. "Rama. I promise you that you're the only one I want."

"Yeah?" He sounds so vulnerable I want to wrap him up and squeeze him until he squeaks, but, instead, I pull him into a soft kiss.

"Okay?" I ask.

"Okay," he says with a nod. When he smiles, it lights up his entire face. And, like always, my heart leaps in answer.

CHAPTER THIRTEEN: Rama

Although I want to, I don't spend the night with Pravat. Something tells me that if I stay, we'll do things that I'd rather save until we aren't so stressed out. It won't be long until we can go on our planned vacation, and I hope for us to get very close during that time. Guarding the tender sprouts of our new relationship has become extremely important to me, and my slight detour into jealous uncertainty over Lin has only strengthened my resolve to make things work.

When I get home, the light is on in my father's study. Before I've turned the deadbolt into place, he appears in the hall.

"It's late. I thought maybe you weren't coming home tonight," he says.

"I went to Pravat's after the fan meeting." Ever since the night he saw me kissing Pravat out on the patio, we haven't spoken about it, but it's always there between us.

He follows me into the living room.

"That's probably for the best."

I turn. "What do you mean?"

"I just think it's wise to be careful," my father says.

"Careful of what?" I ask, rankling. "Oh, you mean of *feelings*. Because I can't possibly have any for a man."

"Calm down, Son. I'm not trying to start an argument."

Taking a deep breath and letting it out, I say more calmly, "Please explain to me why you doubt my feelings for Pravat."

Settling into the chair in the corner, my father answers, "Any new relationship deserves some forethought before it gets to the physical stage."

"What makes you think it hasn't already gotten to that stage?" I ask. A part of me can't believe my audacity, but the need to protect what I have with Pravat is stronger than any embarrassment or shame I might have in front of my father.

He recovers quickly. "Because you aren't gay. You've never been interested in men, so I feel confident you haven't jumped into bed with one. Rama, when you take a moment to step back and look, can't you see that this situation has colored the way you see things?"

"Of course it has," I say. "It's changed everything about the way I see things. How could it not?"

But the pleased expression that suddenly appeared on my father's face leaks away when I continue, "Going into this, I thought I would be acting the part of a man who falls in love with another man and that's all. But very quickly I began to see that love is about who we are inside more than anything else."

"That's all well and good, but it doesn't change the fact that physical attraction is a big part of love," my father says.

I nod in agreement. "Yes, it is."

"Are you saying you're physically attracted to Pravat? A *man*?"

My stomach knots. No matter how strong my feelings are for Pravat and how much I want to guard that, it seems that when it comes right down to it, it isn't so easy admitting to my father that I feel lust for another man. I take so long to answer, I can see the triumph building in his countenance.

Forcing myself to find the courage, I open my mouth and say emphatically, "Yes."

Confusion clouds my father's eyes. "But you can't be. You've dated girl after girl, Rama. I'm not talking about affection, here. I'm talking about—"

I hold up my hand to stop him. "I know what you're talking about, and I'm telling you I feel it."

"Never have you showed even the faintest interest in the same sex!" Pah argues.

"Haven't you ever stopped to wonder why I've never stayed with any girl longer than a couple of months?" I ask.

My father frowns. "I just thought you were picky."

"More like detached. Disconnected. Those girls were a means of physical relief, and that's all. The moment the sex ended, I couldn't wait to be away from them. Is that how you felt with Mah?"

It's as though all the air is sucked from the room. My sister and I never speak about our mother to Pah. Never. Her death was painful to all of us, but my father suffered the worst, locking himself in his study for weeks after it happened, forcing my aunt and uncle to have to care for me and my sister.

I watch as he opens his mouth and shuts it again, face carefully blank except for the hurt shining from his eyes.

"Of course it wasn't."

"It's not the way I feel with Pravat, either," I say. I turn to go to my room, but my father stops me.

"Rama. You need to take into account that you went through a confusing and traumatic experience at an early age. You also...lost your mother. Those things could very well have something to do with the choices you're making now in your love life."

My mouth drops open. "Are you saying you think I've turned to a man for love because of what Aunt Sunnee did to me?" The idea is so disagreeable, I can't quite wrap my mind around it.

"It's not beyond the realm of possibility. Have you told your therapist about your current relationship?"

White hot anger fills me, and I abruptly turn and stalk to my room, shutting the door behind me.

Throwing myself on my bed, I stew for a long time. I haven't told my therapist about my relationship with Pravat, but only because we haven't gotten that far. Talking about what happened to me with Aunt Sunnee has been a long, painful process.

My cell phone rings, and, seeing my agent's name on the screen, I pick up.

"Ace."

"Hi, Rama. I have several advertisers inquiring after you, man. You've become a hot commodity. I'm emailing those I approve of, so you can choose." He curses. "Sorry, I have to go. Traffic's bad. Don't leave it too long, okay? They'll find someone else." He disconnects.

With a sigh, I heave myself from my bed to take a shower.

It isn't until the next day, while I'm scarfing down a sandwich while a staff member puts the final touches on my hair for the next scene that I get a chance to open the emails to see which advertisers want me.

An energy drink. Makeup. Shampoo and conditioner. Skin care. And about a dozen more. I glance through them, choose the ones I'm familiar with and wouldn't feel like a liar advertising, and digitally sign the contracts before sending them on just as Maha walks briskly into the room and waves me out of my chair.

What follows is another long day of filming, but, to our surprise, after wrapping up Maha announces this one is our last.

"I thought we had two more scenes to film?" Pravat says.

"Tida ditched those. We're done. All that's left to film are scenes that don't include either of you."

Lin approaches and hands me and Rama a piece of paper. "Here's your list of promotional events for the next few months as well as the details for the wrap-up party."

I glance over mine before folding it and sticking it into my pocket. Outside the window, it's pitch dark, and I realize another entire day has slipped by while I've been inside this building.

Heaving a sigh, I lean against the wall and close my eyes, suddenly too tired to move, as though now that it knows I'm finished, my body has stopped working entirely.

"Hey," Pravat says, his voice breaking through the buzz of exhaustion that's taken up in my head. He touches my arm. "Rama, we can go home."

With a sigh, I push off the wall, the tired mumbles of goodnight from the crew following us to the elevator.

"The wrap-up party is at the studio this time," Pravat says as we descend to the garage. At the end of the first season, Tida had the cast party at a club. I'm kind of glad we aren't repeating that because it was chaotic and some people attended that I would rather not have seen, namely Preed. "The trailer was released last week. Have you seen it?"

I shake my head.

"I haven't either. No time."

I nod tiredly. The elevator doors slide open, and we step off and into the dimly lit underground garage.

"Come to my place," Pravat says. "In fact, just ride with me. We can pick up your car tomorrow." When I turn to him, he smiles. "You look beat and don't need that long drive."

It isn't a difficult decision to make. Nodding, I climb into the passenger seat of Pravat's Miata and fall asleep before he can even start the engine.

CHAPTER FOURTEEN: Pravat

♥

Rama looks so peaceful asleep in my car that I hate to wake him. Turns out, he barely rouses and I have to half-haul him out of my car and inside the building, his arm slung around my neck.

Good thing I live in a building with full security and a private parking area, or someone would have gotten pictures of us long ago and splashed them all over the internet. As it is, no one but a vaguely curious security guard sees us get onto the elevator, Rama's head sagging onto my shoulder as I press the buttons.

"Sleepy," he murmurs, as cute as a little boy. As the doors slide shut, I kiss his head affectionately. He's never been good at staying awake when he's tired, often napping on my lap between scenes on nights we filmed late. Now, though, he seems particularly exhausted.

Inside my apartment, I help him undress to his shorts and tuck him into bed.

"You not coming?" he murmurs as I sit down on the couch and pick up a book.

"I need to unwind for a while first," I say. I'm exhausted, too, but my mind's going a mile a minute. So much so, that I can't focus on the book and wind up staring at the ceiling, Rama's soft, rumbling snores lulling me into a doze until the sound of my book tumbling to the floor jolts me awake.

Quietly, I undress and slip under the covers, scooting closer to the warmth of Rama's body.

I like having him in my bed. Sud used to practically live with me, but somehow it feels different lying next to Rama. Maybe it's because we don't have sex that makes it so much more—personal. But shouldn't the intimate knowledge of someone else's body be the most personal thing in the world? Yet, somehow, it isn't.

But there's no denying that my feelings for Rama are so much deeper than they ever were for Sud, and, looking back, I know I could not then identify that odd emotion mixed with the heartache when we ended things for what it actually was—*Relief*.

Sud had been too much work. We were happy as boyfriends when at university, but as soon as I started acting, he became this seething ball of jealousy that never let up. I thought letting him see how it's done might help—that as soon as the director called an end to the scene, the romance and sexual charge ended. But Sud saw what he wanted to see, and our relationship slowly crumbled until there was nothing left. Not even friendship.

I haven't seen Sud in a while. He switched majors soon after our breakup, and his faculty building is now across campus from mine rather than next door.

I can't believe I'll graduate in a few months. Not for the first time, I wonder if I made a mistake majoring in dramatic arts. How far is that going to carry me? My career could crash and burn at any moment due to the whims of the bl fan base, and no official words printed on a diploma will help me then. I've sometimes thought I'd like to direct, but I'm still far from that goal.

My thoughts lead to the farce with Lin. Although I don't enjoy the lie, I do feel it has some merit. Since I started being photographed with her, the fan sites' comment sections contain a healthy mix of those who want to see me in a romantic relationship with Rama and those who seem almost relieved to see proof that I'm not.

This isn't the message that I want to project. Don't I, as a member of the LBGT community, have an obligation to make a change? Hell, gay marriage isn't even legal in Thailand, yet we have this lucrative entertainment industry focused on gay relationships—all based on the assumption that the actors playing in them are straight. It doesn't make any fucking sense.

"Are you going to sleep or think all night?" Rama's voice rumbles in the semi-darkness.

"Sorry. Did I wake you?"

"No." Turning over, Rama peers at me through the darkness, the night light behind me casting enough light for me to make out his handsome features. "Is something bothering you?"

I shake my head. Talking about the subject won't do any good. "Just wired for some reason."

He scoots closer, bringing his warmth with him.

"Are you sure?" Long fingers lightly pass over my cheekbone to my nose and then down to trace my mouth.

Without thinking, I take one between my lips, sucking on it gently. Rama's eyes widen, the brown irises deepening to almost black as he pulls in a breath.

"Pravat..."

Letting his finger drop from my mouth, I smile ruefully. "Sorry. Go back to sleep."

"What if I don't want to?" Moving even closer, he aligns his body with mine, hand coming to rest just above where my boxers sit on my hips.

My heartbeat picks up as I wait to see what he'll do.

Leaning in, he takes my bottom lip into his mouth and nibbles on it, sending crazy little darts of need shooting to my groin. I let him lead, languidly moving my mouth against his at every prompt of his lips and tongue.

"Don't you want me?" Rama asks, startling me out of the fog I've fallen into.

Pulling away, I stare into his eyes. I'm shocked at the lack of confidence I see there.

"*Of course* I want you," I say. Taking his hand, I move it to where my cock juts out of my shorts. "Feel how much I want you."

A strangled noise escapes Rama's throat. Pushing the covers from our bodies, he looks down at his hand, curling his fingers around my erection.

Rama returns his gaze to mine. "What do I do?"

"What do you want to do?" I ask, barely able to get the words out because having Rama's hand around my cock is so intensely arousing.

"I want to...I don't know. *Explore*, I guess." He looks at me as though for permission, and I nod.

"Please," I encourage.

His lips press against my clavicle before traveling to latch onto my left nipple, making me suck in a sharp breath. Squeezing my cock in his warm palm, he then brushes his thumb under the head while lightly sinking his front teeth into my nipple.

I nearly come off the bed.

I grasp his hand, stopping all movement and squeezing my eyes shut, heart thundering in my ears.

"Did I do something wrong?" Rama whispers.

"I promise, you're doing everything right. Too right. But I'm about to finish before we even get started." When I open my eyes, he's smiling at me.

"You don't have to look so smug about it," I say, chuckling.

"I've been afraid I won't be able to please you."

I frown, studying Rama's face. "Fuck, Rama. You please me without doing anything at all. I—" Before I can finish the thought, a look of determination takes over his face, and he clamps his mouth over mine, tongue pushing inside while his palm slides over my cock again and again until all thoughts vacate my head. Body thrumming, I can only moan and writhe, unable to stop the momentum as he quickly brings me to climax. And even then he doesn't let up, pulling every last drop from me until I'm a trembling, panting mess.

"Holy shit," I say say on a groan. After a moment, my eyes flutter open and the first thing I see is Rama's boxers bulging in the front with what has to be a painful erection.

Scooting down on the bed, I push his shorts to his thighs and take his pulsing hardness into my mouth. The taste and scent of him overwhelm my senses, shocking life back into my previously spent cock.

Above my head, Rama's making noises that belong in an erotic film as I suck, taking him deeper with every downward motion of my head, enjoying the feel of his soft, heavy balls in my palm. I swallow around him, and he bucks into my mouth, fingers clenching in my hair. Choking slightly, I continue to bob over him.

"Fuck, fuck, fuck!" Rama yells as warm spurts of salty cum hit the back of my throat. I swallow greedily, so lost in him that I continue to suck until he begs me to stop.

Head on Rama's flat stomach, I lie listening to him catch his breath, still buzzing from my own previous orgasm and the sexual high of sucking him off. I'm not sure what was better, to be honest. Giving Rama pleasure was the best kind of high.

But soon the doubts start to gather in my mind. Should I have done that? I hadn't even asked him how he felt about another man sucking his cock.

"Stop," Rama says drowsily, stoking my hair. "I'm fine. Everything's fine."

I can't help but smile. *How does he know?*

I close my eyes.

CHAPTER FIFTEEN: Rama

♥

Privately, I've been hoping that Pete simply forgot to formally ask me to be his best man, but as the date of the wedding comes closer and more news of it trickles down to me from family, I realize that he really isn't going to do it. That hurts more than I'm willing to admit. Pete certainly would have been my choice if the situation were reversed. The fact that he isn't squarely on my side after what I went through last summer is like a knife to the gut.

How could he believe her over me? The knife twists.

On my way to my bedroom, I overhear Chinda on the phone and linger in the doorway of her bedroom until she finishes with the call.

"Was that Sarah?" I ask, although I'm pretty sure it was. Sarah is Pete's sister and a year younger than Chinda.

Chinda nods. "She wanted to know what I'll be wearing to Pete's wedding."

"It's still two months away," I say.

"Uh." Grunting, she shakes her head like I'm hopeless. "We can't wait until the last minute, *duh*."

"Did she tell you who's in the wedding party?" I ask.

A guilty look crosses my sister's face, giving me the answer before she even speaks.

"It's, uh, Mark and Kris for Pete, and Alex's two brothers for him."

Mark and Kris are also our cousins, but neither of them is as close to Pete as I am.

Was.

Pushing off the door frame, I start to leave, but Chinda calls out to me.

"He doesn't really think you're lying."

I turn to look at her where she sits on her bed, twisting the corner of her sheet between her fingers.

"How do you know that?"

"Sarah told me. She says Pete thinks false memories surfaced when you got sick doing your internship in New York."

Got sick is a nice way of putting the breakdown I had when Aunt Sunnee unexpectedly visited Pete and Alex's. And what the hell? *False memories?*

"That's just another way of saying he thinks I'm lying and that I believe my own lies. And why isn't he talking to me? Why didn't he ask me to be in his wedding?"

"She said he's worried about stirring things up and spoiling the wedding for Alex. Both you and Aunt Sunnee will be there, and things will probably be weird. I'm sure he's really anxious about it."

When I don't say anything, Chinda sighs. "You know Uncle Bank isn't in good health. It's one of the reasons Pete and Alex decided to move forward with a wedding."

Pah's youngest brother's poor health is the reason Pete's parents recently moved back to Thailand. I don't doubt it played a large role in Pete and Alex finally setting a date.

"Sorry, but that's not a good reason to stop talking to me and leaving me out of his wedding."

"Pete probably thinks it would upset Aunt Sunnee if you're in the wedding party."

"Fuck Aunt Sunnee!" The anger and frustration burst out of me. At Chinda's stunned expression, I mumble an apology and take refuge in my bedroom.

Barely stopping myself from punching the wall, I tell myself to get a hold of my anger. I've never been one to resort to destructive behavior when upset. Deciding to take more productive action, I pick up my phone and dial Pete's number.

Pacing my bedroom, I listen to an indie band until the call goes to voicemail.

"It's Rama. Call me," I say before disconnecting and tossing my phone on the bed.

Sitting on the edge, I miserably stare down at the carpet, wondering if Pete is the only one in the family who thinks I've made all this up or if others do also. From what I've heard, Sunnee's spread the word about my "false" accusations. Will everyone at the wedding be staring at me, speculating? Maybe Pete's doing me a favor by not asking me to stand up with him. Hell, I could just skip the event altogether. But even as the thought occurs to me, I reject it. I don't want to regret missing Pete and Alex's big moment one day.

Glancing at the clock by my bed, I get to my feet and head to the bathroom. I have to be at the photographer's studio in a little over an hour for the last of the promotional photos for season two.

It doesn't matter what I wear since I'll have to change for the photos, so after my shower I throw on a pair of shorts and a tank and head out for the car. It's hot, and my car's been sitting out in the sun all day, so I crank up the air conditioner.

IN LOVE

When I arrive, Pravat is walking into the building, and I tap my horn to get his attention. Then I realize that Lin is with him. *What the hell? Does she have to go everywhere with him now?*

They stop and wait for me. I do my best to put on a relaxed smile, but I doubt I'm fooling anyone.

We barely have time to exchange greetings because the photographer's assistants are on us as soon as we're inside the door, corralling us into changing rooms to get ready for the first shoot.

The theme is *bad boy*, and I have so much kohl around my eyes, I feel ridiculous. I nearly swallow my tongue when Pravat appears wearing a black leather jacket and matching pants with his black hair in spikes and his chest bare.

The heated way Pravat looks at me has me glancing at the mirror on the wall. Besides the kohl, I'm wearing black jeans, a crisp, white, over-sized shirt strategically buttoned wrong and sliding off my shoulder, and six silver rings attached to my left ear. I'm also barefoot. Pravat wears heavy black boots.

Since the moment we were paired together, I have been portraying the softer side of our couple. And I don't mind. In fact, I find that I like it. It's weird, because I don't think I necessarily put off "wife" vibes, as the fans call it. The thought of taking this role with any other man doesn't sit well with me, but with Pravat, it seems right.

For the first picture, the photographer poses Pravat leaning back against a black motorcycle, one knee bent and his arm wrapped loosely around my waist as I stand in front of him. Before backing away to his camera, he adjusts Pravat's hand so that it lifts my shirt in the front, gently resting just above my jeans. The warmth of his palm raises goosebumps on my skin.

"Good. Now, Rama, let's see you smolder and pout," the photographer directs.

Somehow, I manage to pull this off. I'm certain that without Pravat there I'd never be able to.

After several shots this way with the photographer—whose name is Noh—murmuring his approval, we are posed again, this time with my back against the brick wall and Pravat leaning into me, holding my wrists above my head with one hand, his nose nearly touching mine as we stare into each other's eyes. Pravat doesn't have on as much makeup as I do, but the little bit of eyeliner he wears make his dark eyes seem menacing as he stares me down. It takes my breath away, and if it weren't for the constant flash of the camera, I'd forget all about the photo shoot.

"Let your mouth fall open, Rama, that's it," the photographer says after a few moments. "Now, wet your bottom lip. Oh, yeah. Just. Like. That." More flashes.

The growl that issues from Pravat's throat goes straight to my cock, and suddenly I'm panting through my parted lips, remembering how it felt to have his mouth on mine. Pravat looks like he wants to shove me into the nearest closet and rip my clothes off, and I don't think it's all for the camera.

"Fabulous," Noh says, taking more pictures. "You guys are hot as hell together."

The next pose has Pravat standing behind me again, this time biting my bare shoulder, and then Noh seats us on the motorcycle. Before I know it, the shoot is over.

"You guys did great," Lin says when when I emerge from the dressing room in my clothes again, face cleaned of makeup.

I'd forgotten she was there. My body still thrums from the intensity of the photo shoot.

"Dinner?" Pravat suggests, joining us.

I'm tempted to say no, but that would leave Pravat and Lin to go alone, and *that's* not happening.

"Sure," I say.

The three of us head out of the building.

CHAPTER SIXTEEN: Lin

The after-party for *In Love* is held in the studio common room. As the last few guests trickle out, the remaining actors and crew begin to clean up. I'm a little sorry for the series to end because I've enjoyed working for Tida a lot more than I imagined I would—and not just because I got to be arm candy for a hot guy. I really enjoyed seeing the ins and outs of filming—something my producer father has never been able to entice me into.

Ying, the makeup assistant, and I begin stuffing paper plates and cups into a giant trash bag.

"Do you think they're really together?" she asks in a low voice.

"Who?" I ask, looking up.

She jerks her head toward where Rama and Pravat sit on the couch, heads together as they look at Pravat's phone. Why would she be asking me, someone who is supposedly dating Pravat, if Rama and Pravat are a couple?

Ying's dark hair ripples over her shoulders as she bends to pick up a piece of cake someone squashed on the floor with their shoe. "If those two aren't together for real, I'll eat my hat."

"It's fanservice," I say.

"Oh, really? Please tell me, then. Where are the *fans*?"

"They're just really good friends, Ying." I feign annoyance. "Do I have to remind you that Pravat and I are seeing each other?"

Ying grunts. "You couldn't be that delusional. I know you'd like to think you and Pravat could have something, but if my man looked at another guy that way, I'd take the hint and move on."

I glance back to the couch. Pravat probably doesn't think he has to be careful with so few people around at the moment, but some of these crew members are gossipers, and the way he's looking at Rama is so damned obvious.

"Haven't you ever heard of bromance?" I mumble.

Ying snorts.

When Tida hired me to help out with odd jobs, she asked me to keep my eyes and ears open. For months, I've been dutifully noting who is and isn't loyal to Hearts Productions. I wouldn't necessarily call Ying disloyal, but Tida doesn't need the gossip. I need to nip this in the bud.

"You're seeing things. I'll show you you're wrong." I wash my hands with sanitizer gel from the table, then walk over to the couch.

"Hi, guys. Fun party, wasn't it?" Winking at Pravat, I settle on his lap, and, under the guise of nuzzling his neck, whisper that people are watching and speculating about him and Rama. His arms come around me, and Rama subtly puts some space between himself and Pravat on the couch. I don't have to check to know Ying's snapping photos with her phone, probably hoping to catch a look of jealousy on Rama's face so she can post it on a website or, worse, sell it to the press. Fortunately, the man has a natural poker face and has become absorbed in his own phone.

For a long time, I sit stroking Pravat's broad chest, taking in the mingling scents of his musky cologne and male sweat. What I'm doing isn't exactly a hardship, but as I'm actually *not* delusional, I know there's absolutely nothing for me to get out of this. Pravat and Rama are as in love as any two people I've ever seen.

Murmuring something about going to the bathroom, Rama eventually gets up and walks off.

"Sorry," I whisper to Pravat. "Ying's sure you two are together."

"You're only doing what P'Tida asked you to do," Pravat says softly. "Don't worry about it." To anyone else, it appears we are whispering cute couple things to each other. *I wish.* He gives me a little half-smile that sends my heart skittering because, hey, I'm only human.

Pravat's phone pings, and from my vantage point, I can clearly see the text from Tida. I don't mean to, but I can't help reading it.

> Take Lin to your place tonight. The press is outside.

Raising my eyes, I catch Pravat's troubled look before he wipes his expression clean.

"Sorry," I say again.

Nudging me off his lap, Pravat stands. "I'm beat. Let's go home."

The place is almost empty now. Clasping my hand in his, he says his goodbyes to the cleaning crew, and we head for the corridor.

In the hall, Rama stands talking to a couple of girls who came with crew members and are practically draped all over him. Spotting us, he raises his hand to wave casually as we walk by them on our way to the elevator.

Once the doors close, Pravat's smile fades to a tight, grim line, and he quickly taps out a text on his phone—I assume to Rama to explain why we're leaving together.

Outside, humidity settles around us like a heavy blanket. It's past midnight, but Bangkok is lit up and pulsing with life. I'm caught off guard when several reporters appear out of nowhere, shooting questions at us as we walk to Pravat's car.

"Pravat! Did the cast party just end? Where's Rama? Lin, isn't it? Is it true you're the daughter of movie producer Chakan Vithoon Sukbunsung? How long have you and Pravat been dating? Where are you headed?"

I keep my head down while Pravat makes a polite, innocuous statement about the cast party being a lot of fun and how he is going to miss the cast and crew, all while continuing to guide me to his car.

"Do you think it's really necessary for me to spend the night?" I once inside his Miata.

"It's probably a good idea." Pravat starts the car and pulls away from the curb just as Rama walks out of the building with the same two girls he was talking to upstairs. Pravat's eyes track them as they round the building to a side parking lot.

"It's good for him to be seen with them by the press," I say. "Otherwise, there might be rumors that he's mooning after you."

Pravat cuts his eyes to me.

"Yes, I know there's something going on between the two of you," I say. "You can trust me."

"Does P'Tida know?"

"If she does, she didn't say it outright. What you do is your own business."

"Is it?" Pravat asks.

I frown. "Yes, I would think so. The series is over now. Do what you want as long as you're discreet."

"It's never that simple," Pravat says.

I fall silent, wondering what he means. Although my father is in the business, I don't know a lot about the film industry, and, from what I've seen, the bl industry has its own unique brand of complications. There isn't anything I can say to make the situation any easier, so I resolve to just get through the night as best I can.

CHAPTER SEVENTEEN: Pravat

♥

I can't stop thinking about Rama leaving the party with those women, which is pretty hypocritical considering I brought Lin home to stay at my place. But Tida told me to do it, *dammit*! Rama *knows* it's just for show, whereas he voluntarily left with those girls.

Do you think he'll do anything with them? I ask myself. *Until he met me, his life was so much simpler. He might decide I'm not worth the trouble.*

Worried that he's going to come to his senses and break things off with me, I stop pretending to straighten up my apartment and turn to Lin.

"I'm going for a short walk to help me sleep. Please make yourself at home."

I know I'm being rude, but I can't help it. I can't get my mind off Rama and those women. Leaving my apartment with my cell phone in hand, I pause in the hallway to glance at it. It hasn't vibrated since I sent the text to Rama earlier explaining about Tida. I'm dismayed to see the text didn't send, and this entire time, Rama has been clueless as to why I took Lin home with me.

I take the stairs to the lobby, and by the time I reach the lit street outside my building, I'm listening to Rama's phone ringing, fear building inside me. He's not going to answer, either because he's angry with me or because he's...busy.

I curse when I get his voicemail, then dial again. And again. I'm just about to run back upstairs for the keys to my car when he picks up.

"It's about time you answered," I say gruffly, way past rationality at this point.

"I was in the shower," Rama says.

Feeling like a fool, I let out a breath and take a moment to pull myself together.

"Pravat?"

Closing my eyes, I confess, "P'Tida told me to take Lin to my place for the night so the press would see us. I didn't want to. I sent you a text but just found out it didn't go through. I panicked. And I saw you with those two women."

The silence on the other end of the phone lasts way too long. When it finally breaks, I can't believe what I'm hearing.

"Are you *laughing*?"

Rama snorts. "Sorry, but you're just so cute. What did you think, I went off somewhere to have sex with two women?"

"I didn't know what to think." I rub my eyes. "Honestly, I was more afraid you're having second thoughts about us."

Rama sighs, and something in the sound makes my stomach tighten.

Falling back against the warm brick of the building, I ask, "*Are* you? Having second thoughts?"

Before he can answer, my eyes land on a car I recognize parked across the street. "Dammit."

"What?" Rama asks.

"There's a reporter watching me. He's probably wondering why I've left my *girlfriend* upstairs to go outside to make a phone call. Fuck, I hate this so much." Turning, I walk inside the building, giving the night guard a friendly nod as I stride toward the elevators.

Rama's voice is soothing. "Listen, don't worry about anything tonight. Everything's fine."

"Everything's *not* fucking fine," I say, stabbing at the button for my floor and glaring at the elevator doors until they shut. "I want to see you. I want *you* in my apartment right now, not Lin. Hell, Rama, when am I going to be able to live my damn life?" I groan, suddenly remembering. "And I've got a fucking exam tomorrow I haven't studied for."

"Prav, listen to me. I'm jealous, okay? I know you don't have any interest in Lin, but I feel the same as you do. I want to be the one there with you. But we can't do anything about this right now, so please just calm down, get some sleep, and when you wake up in the morning, study for your exam." He pauses. "Lin's going to sleep on the couch, right?"

"I thought I'd give her my bed, and I'll sleep on the couch," I say wearily.

"Okay. I guess."

I chuckle in spite of myself. "I'll change the sheets tomorrow."

"Yeah. You do that," he says tightly, and the tension that's been coiled in my gut releases a little bit.

We say goodnight, and I return to my apartment to find Lin wearing one of my T-shirts and lying in what I've come to think of as Rama's place on my bed.

"Sorry," she says. "I didn't know what to put on. I saw this on top of your dresser.

"That's fine." I shut and lock the door.

"Is everything okay?"

"Yeah." Placing my phone on the bar, I ask, "You want something to eat?"

"No, I ate plenty at the party. I'm just going to sleep, if that's okay with you."

"Of course." I'm relieved I don't have to make small talk with her.

In the bathroom, I brush my teeth and change into a shirt and sleep pants, then lie down on the couch, silently going over my phone conversation with Rama.

Before I spotted that reporter, was Rama going to tell me he was having second thoughts about us? Is being with me too difficult for him? And what about the future? We may be finished with this series, but there will be others. Tida might decide it would be better not to pair us up again. Work is work but imagining Rama doing fanservice with another actor does make me a little jealous.

Or Rama might decide he doesn't want to do another boys' love drama. He might take a romantic lead opposite a woman instead. That would be even worse—I don't have the equipment to compete with a woman.

I give myself a mental nudge. I should be concentrating on graduating in July, not worrying over my love life. I'm going to have to get a good night's sleep, so I can concentrate on studying in the morning. Hopefully, Lin will go home early. Closing my eyes, I concentrate on the quiet soughs coming from the bed, wishing they were Rama's soft snores and I were there beside him, until I finally drift off.

CHAPTER EIGHTEEN: Rama

♥

"Rama."

I'm so surprised to hear Pete's voice, I'm struck dumb for a moment.

"You there?"

"Yeah," I say. "I didn't think you'd return my call, and my screen said *Alex*."

Silence, and then, "I'm borrowing his phone. Sorry I didn't call sooner. I just—hell, I don't know. This has all been really difficult."

Tell me about it.

"Congratulations on setting a date," I say tightly.

"Uh, thanks. With Uncle Bank's health and all, we thought we'd better do it. I, uh, just..." he trails off.

"You just wish it wasn't coming at the heels of this mess with Aunt Sunnee," I finish for him.

Pete sighs. "Yeah."

I walk out to the pool area, so I can't be overheard by Pah and Chinda.

"You really believe her over me? I swear, Pete, it happened. I just tried to forget about it, but when she suddenly appeared at your place, it all came back to me."

I listen to Pete's breathing for a moment before he says, "She really...touched you? Like, in a sexual way? Are you sure—"

"Yes. I'm positive. You want the details?" I ask, stomach cramping. If I have to give them to him, I'm going to throw up.

"No. No, I don't. I don't want you to have to repeat it."

"I'm not lying," I say.

"Okay."

"Okay, what? Okay you believe me or okay you want me to stop saying it?"

"I don't know what to believe, Rama. I never expected this. Aunt Sunnee has always been so nice to me."

"She was always nice to me, too, until she got into my bed and touched me!" I say loudly, then look over my shoulder to make sure nobody inside the house heard.

"Okay, okay. But I couldn't just leave her off the guest list."

"I didn't say you should."

"Is it going to be weird for you with her there?"

"What do you think?" I ask angrily, then take a deep breath. "Maybe I shouldn't go." I don't mean it, not really, although part of me yearns to take the easy way out.

"I'd understand if you didn't."

It's like a splash of cold water to the face.

"Fuck you, Pete," I say and hang up.

To Pete's credit, he tries calling me back, but I don't answer. I'm already late to the taping of a promotional show. Rather than going through the house and having to face Pah or Chinda, I exit through the gate and walk around to the garage to get my car.

As I drive, anger rages inside me. I didn't miss the relief in Pete's voice when he thought I might back out of going to the wedding. Well, fuck that. I'm the victim in this. I'm not going to let everyone think I can't face them because I've told some vindictive lie. Aunt Sunnee should be the one not to go. How she can pretend she's innocent is beyond me.

Niggling doubt eats away at me. What if...but *no*. I did *not* imagine what happened during that trip. I've talked to my therapist many times about this, and she's helped me to see that it's natural to doubt myself, and that, unfortunately, victims are blamed. It's fucking unfair, but it happens all the time. During our last session, I brought up the doubts my father introduced in my mind about why I'm attracted to Pravat. Talking about it helps, but nothing can make up for the fact that Pravat and I can't be together like we want.

The parking lot at the department store where Pravat and I are filming a promotion for a skin care line is teeming with cars when I pull in, but I have the code for the underground parking garage, and soon I'm riding the elevator to the second floor where I'm greeted by a smartly dressed woman with a bright smile.

"Hello, Mr. Sathianthai. I'm Gail. We spoke on the phone. Come this way. Mr. Benjawan is already here."

I spot him sitting at a long table covered in pink silk with an array of products artfully set out in front of him. I have a second to admire him in the baby blue jacket with the cosmetic company's emblem on the chest before our eyes meet, and he smiles that smile that always seems just for me.

"If you could put this on," Gail says, holding up an identical jacket. As I slip into it, my eyes meet Pravat's and a spark of electricity zips between us.

The afternoon goes by quickly. Pravat and I flirt easily while discussing the skincare products. Department store security as well as the security from Hearts Entertainment hold back the crowd around us.

At one point, Pravat and I, our hair pulled back in whimsical hair bands, are coerced into applying revitalizing masks to each other's faces. Pravat looks adorable with panda ears on his head, and he keeps calling me "bunny" due to my pink rabbit ears. The crowd loves this kind of thing, and we good-naturedly play up to their encouragement.

When the two-hour event ends, I smile and wave to the fans as I walk to the back hall with Pravat.

"What are you smiling about?" He asks me fondly after we say our goodbyes to the event handlers and make our way to the parking garage.

I shrug. "That was fun."

"It was," he agrees. Touching his cheek, he adds, "And my skin is silky soft."

I laugh. We reach my car first, and Pravat lingers a moment.

"We don't have anything going for the next week until the premiere of episode one," he says. "Let's go away together. To the beach."

I grin. "Just the two of us? Alone together?"

Grinning back, Pravat nods. "Yeah. Pack tonight. I'll make all the arrangements."

I can't think of a reason to say no. Not that I want to, but will it really be that easy? Can we simply pack up and drive off together for a relaxing week with no eyes on us?

"Okay," I say, a slow smile spreading across my face.

"It might be best if we meet someplace, and then I'll drive us. I'll text you the details later."

The muscles in my abdomen tighten in anticipation. "Okay," I say before ducking into my car.

· ♥ · ♥ · ♥ · ♥ · ♥ ·

"Rama, where are you going?"

I place my bag in the trunk of my car and slam it closed before turning to face my father.

"I'm going to the beach for a week. I thought you were still at work. I was going to text you."

Pah's eyes are unreadable. "You're going with Pravat."

"Yes."

He shakes his head, a stiff, curt movement. In the light of the sinking sun, the strands of gray in his dark hair stand out, and his face looks haggard.

"Maybe it's for the best. You'll see you're making a mistake," he says.

I start to tell him he's wrong but stop myself, knowing there's no point. He can think what he wants.

"I'll be back Sunday night," I say and climb into the car to drive to Pravat's friend Kiet's apartment where I'll be leaving my car this week as my house is in the other direction from where Pravat and I will be traveling.

I don't realize how tense I am until Pravat looks me over with a frown.

"You okay?" he asks.

I nod. "Let's get out of here."

As soon as we're underway, Pravat takes my hand.

"Feels good to get away, doesn't it?"

"Yeah. It really does."

I don't tell him how irritated my father made me before I left because I'm already feeling better than I have in weeks just knowing we're escaping for a while.

The last thing I want to do is to fall asleep, but the next thing I know, Pravat is waking me with a gentle shake to the shoulder, and I open my eyes to swaying palm trees and briney ocean air wafting in from the open window.

"I'm sorry for konking out on you," I say, rubbing my eyes and stretching.

"Don't be. I'm glad you got some rest."

I smile ruefully. "But you didn't."

"I'm totally caught up on sleep. Don't worry about it." Unbuckling his seatbelt, Pravat shoots a sexy smile at me before climbing out of the car.

Outside, the air is a good ten degrees cooler than it had been in Bangkok and much less humid. I take in a deep breath, looking out at the ocean in the dim light of the rising moon.

"Where's the hotel?" I ask.

"Kiet's father owns those bungalows over there." Pravat points to a row of low buildings in the distance and holds up a key. "Ours is the second one."

"Really? That's awesome!" I suddenly realize how much more comfortable and private our own bungalow will be compared to a hotel room.

My eyes flick to Pravat's full bottom lip. I suddenly want to kiss him so badly I can't stand it. But although no one's around, we shouldn't take chances. Being in the bl industry puts us in the odd position of being rock star famous to some while completely anonymous to many others. It's easy to lower our guard, but all we need is for one fan to see us, and our relationship will be all over the entertainment news. For this reason, we both have donned dark sunglasses and baseball caps.

"Let's get settled in the bungalow," I say, hefting my bag out of Pravat's trunk. We walk toward the row of bungalows ahead, the sound of the ocean at our backs.

Our unit is small but cozy with a pull-out bed sporting a surprisingly comfortable mattress where we immediately curl up together after separately showering off the day's grime and changing into fresh clothes. It still strikes me as strange how comfortable I feel in Pravat's arms. He's a haven to me I never thought I would have, and no matter what happens between us in the future, I'm always going to be grateful for that.

Running his fingertip over my lips, Pravat says solemnly, "I love you."

I hold his gaze, only lowering my lids as he presses his lips to mine. His mouth tastes of the sweet soda he was drinking in the car, and I lick it from every corner, pressing into him eagerly, the realization that we're not going to be interrupted making me bold.

The feel of his bare legs brushing against mine sends tiny pinpricks of awareness throughout my body.

"You taste so good," he says against my lips before moving downward and nibbling at my neck just above my tank top.

Pushing him backward onto the bed, I kiss his soft mouth. His slick, agile tongue slides against mine—so different from the way we kiss on film. Recently, during a kissing scene, I almost forgot and slipped my tongue inside his mouth. That would have been embarrassing and difficult to explain. When we come up for air, my heart's beating fast and hard and my erection is straining against my zipper.

"Tell me what you want," Pravat says, looking at me so hungrily I feel a blush climbing up my neck.

"What do *you* want?" I ask.

"I want everything you're willing to give right now," he says earnestly.

"Do you want to fuck me?"

Pravat stares at me. "Uh..."

"Or maybe you want, uh, me to..." I'd always assumed I would be the bottom, but maybe Pravat...images of sinking inside his body scramble my brain, and it takes me a moment to pull my thoughts together.

"I've never bottomed," Pravat says. "But if that's what you want, I can try it."

"Maybe this is weird for a guy who's only been with women," I say, "but I think I want to be on the bottom. At least, the first time."

I watch his Adam's apple bob as he swallows.

"Yeah? Okay. But we don't have to do anything like that now."

"I want to," I say, wondering at myself. Am I crazy? I have absolutely no idea what I'm getting into. But I do know that I trust Pravat. Curling my fingers into his shirt, I tug him forward and kiss him with everything I've got.

CHAPTER NINETEEN:

Pravat

♥

After kissing me hard enough to curl my toes, Rama explains why he wants to bottom for me.

"I know it will hurt, but I just want to feel you holding me down, deep inside me—"

With a harsh expulsion of breath, I squeeze my aching cock beneath the fabric of my shorts. "Stop, Rama. Stop," I beg.

A smile plays about his sensuous mouth. "You like the sound of that, huh?"

I close my eyes. "Don't tease me."

Rama's fingers trail down to my stomach. "I'm not teasing. I really want this."

Feeling the bed dip, I open my eyes to the sight of Rama stripping off his shirt. When he unzips his shorts, I have to squeeze my cock again.

"I, uh, I...I..." I can't form a single coherent thought.

"Did you bring any lube?" he asks.

Holy shit. "Rama, are you sure you want to—"

He meets my eyes. "I'm sure. Did you?"

I point to my bag.

Rama slides off the bed, losing his shorts in the process, and moves to my open bag on the table.

"Side pocket," I say, squeezing my hard cock. *How am I going to last?*

"Strip," Rama tells me.

As I obey, I wonder how the hell he can be so calm. Aren't I the one who should be taking the lead?

But when he returns to the bed, naked and with a liberal amount of the clear jelly on his fingers, I can see the nervousness in his eyes, and that's all it takes to get rid of my uncertainty.

"I think it would be easier if you let me do that part."

Rama raises horrified eyes to me. "What?"

"Come here." I tug him down so he's lying on top of me and kiss him until he relaxes.

"I...If you..." Rama begins.

"Please don't say that if I were a woman, you would know what to do," I say.

"Sorry." Rama lowers his eyes. "Shit, I've gotten this stuff all over you." He wipes at the lube on my chest.

"It's okay," I say, stilling his hand. I pull him into another kiss, lapping my tongue over his lips before delving inside his mouth until he sinks sweet and compliant against me. Only then do I swipe my finger into the puddle on my chest and move my hand down between the cheeks of his ass.

Rama stiffens when my finger circles his puckered opening. "Oh, *fuck.*"

"I won't do anything until you're ready," I say, and kiss down his throat, my erection stiff between us. Rama's soft skin rubbing against the head is about to drive me insane.

When he begins to rut against me, I tap his hole and whisper, "Ready?"

At his nod, I gently press the tip of my finger inside him.

"Okay?" I ask, surprised when he barely tenses up.

In answer, he turns his head and kisses me hard, biting at my lips until I forget what I'm doing and get lost in kissing him back.

"I want you inside me," he whispers.

"I have to make sure you can take me," I say, slowly adding a second finger.

Rama gasps. I work him open for a long time before adding a third digit.

"Oh, shit," he says on a moan.

Taking a steadying breath, I grab the bottle of lube and put some more on my fingers. This time, after a few moments of kissing, I slide them farther into his tight, hot passage and spread them a little.

Rama cries out, breath warm against my ear as his body clamps down on me.

I kiss his shoulder, then his lips, slowly rotating my fingers inside him.

He winces, but, after a few seconds, relaxes, chest rising and falling with rapid pants as I zero in on his prostate. His whimper almost does me in. Stopping what I'm doing, I take several deep breaths and let them out.

Rama rises to his knees, and I gasp when he straddles me and takes my cock in his hand to rub the head against his hole. With a look of determination, he begins to sink onto me.

I'm not what you'd call huge, but I'm not small either, and I know this has to hurt. Sud cried the first time we did it. But Rama steadfastly continues, a fine layer of sweat appearing on his pale skin, until his ass touches my thighs.

"Fu-uck," I whisper in tortured pleasure.

Rama swallows, his chest rising and falling rapidly as he adjusts.

"It feels...it feels so full." He takes a deep breath and lets it out. "So good." A smile blooms on his face. "I like it."

I can only moan in answer, my cock encased in the hot vise of his body. I'm afraid to move or I'll blow.

Suddenly, something occurs to me. "Rama, we should have used a condom. There're some in my bag."

"I don't want one," Rama says, fingers inching up my torso to tweak my nipples, making me jerk inside him. I can't help but laugh at how his eyes widen.

"That's what you get," I tell him before my expression turns serious. "We really should use a condom."

"Nothing short of the ceiling falling down on us is going to get me off your cock," Rama says stubbornly. Expression softening, he adds, "I'm clean. I promise you. I'm too OCD not to be tested regularly."

I believe that, but there's another problem.

"I haven't been tested since right after Sud and I broke up."

"But he's the only one you've been with, right?"

"Like *this*, yeah. But I've done other stuff. I mean, it's probably okay, but—"

Rama ends the debate by rising up my shaft and then slowly sinking back down onto it.

We both moan, and, as he sets a grueling pace, I completely forget everything else.

"Rama, wait. Rama...Rama..." His name becomes a litany from my lips as he drives me higher and higher.

Seeing he isn't going to let up, I brace my feet on the bed and thrust up into him, taking his half-hard cock in my still-slick hand and pumping to our rhythm.

"I can't...I'm going to..." Rama's head falls back and he groans, beads of sweat rolling down his chest.

I don't remember it ever being this good. Sure, there was desire and release, but not this connection pulling me under, making me want more, harder, faster.

Tug, twist, tug, twist. The rosy tip of Rama's long cock pops up between my thumb and pointer finger again and again, bringing him closer and closer to the edge, his body tightening around mine until, suddenly, I seize with pleasure. My eyes flutter shut as a hundred light bulbs shatter in front of them. A broken sound escapes Rama's throat and warm liquid splatters my hand. His ass contracts around my cock, sucking me dry until I grab his hips, stilling his movements, my back arching off the sweat-drenched bed.

"Careful," I say, wincing as he rises off me, my spent cock slapping my stomach with a wet sound.

"Be right back," Rama says and rushes to the bathroom.

When a few minutes go by and he hasn't appeared, I call out, "You okay?"

The toilet flushes and then I hear water running before he walks out and dives onto the bed with me, kissing all over my chest.

"I'm good," he says, smiling up at me.

I study his face. "You sure?"

"Mmhmm," he murmurs, curling into me like a kitten. "That was perfect."

Petting his hair, I whisper, "Yes, it definitely was."

CHAPTER TWENTY: Rama

We sleep the night and half the next day only to finally drag ourselves out of bed and realize we don't have any food in the bungalow. So, we head out to a local restaurant where we can eat seafood on a large covered porch overlooking the ocean.

"This is amazing," I say on a sigh, leaning back in my chair, hand over my full stomach. I'm a little sore but do my best to hide it from Pravat. Nothing I ever experienced before could compare with the feeling of having him inside me. I've found myself spacing out several times already thinking about it that morning.

Sitting across from me, Pravat looks incredibly handsome in his jeans, skin like honey against his sky-blue shirt. He keeps giving me small, secret smiles that make my heart dance.

"You're amazing."

I laugh, heat rising into my face. Looking back out to sea, I say, "I guess we should go pick up some groceries before we head back to the bungalow."

"Sounds good."

We pay the bill. As I stand outside waiting while Pravat visits the men's room, I spot a familiar face.

Is that...? No, it couldn't be.

"Ready?" Pravat says from behind me.

"Look," I say, pointing to the lot beside the restaurant.

Pravat squints into the sun. "What? Wait, is that...Mint?"

"You don't think...he followed us?"

"Only one way to find out." Pravat starts across the parking lot, me at his heels.

The closer we get, the more I'm sure it's Mint. I recognize his jacket. He disappears around a building.

"Do you think he's spying on us?" I ask as we hurry across the small median of grass that separates the two parking lots.

"I don't trust him," Pravat says. When we barrel around the building, he abruptly stops, I slam into him, falling backward onto my ass.

Dazed, I look up, and it takes my brain a minute to catch up to what I'm seeing.

Mint. And...and *Two*? Locked in a fierce kiss.

Sensing our presence, Mint and Two shoot apart.

Turning and completely blocking the man behind him from our view, Mint stares at us.

"What the fuck?"

In that moment it's perfectly clear Mint had no idea we were there. "What are you two doing here?" he demands.

"We were going to ask you the same thing," Pravat says as I brush sand off my ass.

"We're...rehearsing," Mint says. Behind him, Two looks shell-shocked.

I want to ask, *For what, porn?*

"What are you two doing here together?" Mint points between me and Pravat.

"We're on vacation," Pravat says easily.

"Yeah, well, so are we," Mint says, then winces as though he'd like to stuff the words back into his mouth and swallow them.

"Guess it's true what they say about there being a fine line between love and hate," I can't resist saying.

"What? Fucking hell," Mint mutters, rubbing his eyes. "That's not what—listen, if you know what's good for you, you'll keep your mouths shut about this."

"No need for threats," Pravat says, voice hardening.

The stark vulnerability on Two's face prompts me to walk over to where Mint still seems to be trying to hide him and ask, "You okay?"

"Of course he's okay," Mint says irritably.

I meet Two's gaze, and in his eyes I see it clearly: He's in love with Mint. The poor bastard.

"I guess we can all agree this never happened," Pravat says, and, turning, takes me by the arm and guides me back around the building to the parking lot.

"That was a surprise," I say.

"No kidding. I was sure he followed us. I never expected to see *that*."

We climb into his car.

"I just hope Two's only having a fling. Mint's not the type to make a new man of himself," Pravat says.

"I think Two likes him." I wrinkle my nose. "How, though? I mean, I can understand a physical attraction, but anything more? I just don't get it. Unless Mint's hiding some totally different personality we don't know about."

Pravat gives me an odd look. "You think Mint's hot?"

"What? No, I just meant...wait. Are you jealous?"

"Yes, I'm jealous!"

I can't help it—I break into laughter. The thought of Pravat being jealous of *Mint* of all people is just too funny.

I swallow my laugh when, with a noise close to a growl, Pravat jerks me over the gear shift and kisses me hard. *Damn.* When we part, I can only stare at him while my mental faculties try to catch up.

A little like the way Two had been staring at Mint earlier.

Pravat's dark eyes flare like he's warning me that the kiss was only the beginning. He starts the car, and I spend the next ten minutes thrumming with wired anticipation because Pravat totally bypasses the store and heads for the bungalow.

Behind closed doors, we grapple, pulling each other's clothes off before falling onto the bed, kissing while desperately rubbing against each other until, with one final surge, my climax hits, sending me soaring. Pravat's body tenses and he lets out a long moan as he follows me over the edge.

Messy but content, we lie on the tangled sheets, naked bodies molded together as we catch our breath. Pravat closes his eyes, and I watch the late afternoon sun play over his golden skin, mind turning again to Mint and Two. I still can't believe it. Has Mint been covering something that's always been there, or was he blindsided by sudden feelings for Two? As I can't imagine ever having a heart-to-heart with Mint, I'll probably never know.

Rolling over carefully so as not to waken Pravat, who is now snoring softly, I fish my phone out of the pocket of my jeans and scroll through my emails. Spotting one from my agent, I open it and read. He wants to see me in his office as soon as possible. *To hell with that.*

I type out a quick reply that I'm out of town for a week and will contact him when I get back to Bangkok and toss my phone onto the floor before curling into the crook of Pravat's arm and closing my eyes.

CHAPTER TWENTY-ONE:

Pravat

♥

After that, our vacation seems to speed up, the days flying by. After having restrained ourselves for so long, Rama and I spend the majority of our time exploring one another in bed. On the few occasions we do go out, we don't see Mint and Two again.

"Maybe we're shooting ourselves in the foot," Rama says as we sit on the beach looking at the stars on our last night there.

"What do you mean?" I ask.

"After this, how are we going to go back to the way it was?"

"The series is over. Contractually, we don't have to hide anymore." I've been giving this a lot of thought but haven't come to any perfect conclusion. I want to be with Rama, but I have to support myself, and, right now, my career is in the bl industry. We both know that if we reveal ourselves as a couple, it will close a lot of doors for both of us.

"So, I don't have to pretend to be dating Lin anymore. But we need to be careful in public. There's always going to be speculation—we can't control that—but we don't want to add wood to the flame."

"Will we accept roles with other people?" Rama asks after a moment of staring at the tide creeping up the shore.

"P'Tida may team us up again in another series."

"Or she might separate us if she thinks we're together," Rama says.

Taking his hand, I tug him closer. "She might. But she can't deny our chemistry or that the fans want to see more of us together. If we're discreet, she may choose to ignore it. I'm sure she already suspects, anyway." I kiss his head. "What are your plans for the next few months?" I ask, changing the subject.

"I've signed with some advertisers," Rama says.

"Really? How many?"

He thinks a moment. "Six. No, seven."

I stare at him.

He frowns. "What?"

"Seven? At once?"

"Is that too many?"

"Yes! You're going to be working your ass off. Didn't Ace tell you to keep it to two or three at most?"

Rama shakes his head.

"You haven't signed contracts, have you?"

He makes a cringing face.

Flopping onto my back in the sand, I stare up at the moon. "We'll be lucky if we ever see each other."

Rama pokes me in the side. "Come on. It can't be that bad."

I wish for his sake that it wasn't, but he's unknowingly signed himself up for a lot of work.

"What about you? What do you plan to do after graduation?" Rama asks.

"Paint while going to auditions. Unless P'Tida comes up with something for us."

"I hate the thought of you playing opposite another man," Rama says.

"You know how impersonal it really is," I say.

"What, from my experience with you? Or from Mint and Two?"

I can't help but laugh. "Okay, I get your point. But this isn't normal, believe me."

Rama rolls to lie on top of me, the moon shining brightly behind his head, illuminating my face while casting his in shadow. "All I know is how easy it's always been with you." He kisses me, lips soft and warm, and we lose ourselves for a long time, the sound of the wind and surf in our ears. Finally, we pull ourselves up and go inside where Rama surprises me by falling to his knees and unzipping my shorts.

When he takes me into his warm mouth, I whisper, "Fuck."

After a moment, he pulls off to take a breath, looking up at me.

"Good?" he asks before immediately sucking my cock back into his mouth. All I can do is groan and tug at his hair. I move my fingers to his jaw, feeling the suction of his cheeks and, without meaning to, pump my hips, choking him.

"Sorry, sorry." I wipe the tears that have welled in his eyes with my thumbs.

Giving me a reproachful look, he goes back to what he was doing, and before long, I'm tugging at his shirt, trying to warn him, but he ignores me.

"Fu-uck," I say reverently as he drinks me down.

Settling back on his heels with a smug look on his handsome face, he says, "The more I do that, the more I like it."

"You're awfully good at it," I tell him, tucking my cock back into my shorts.

Smiling, he gets up and flops down on the bed, picking up his phone from the side table.

"I have a text from Chinda," he says, sitting up. His face goes white as a sheet.

"What's wrong?" I ask as he puts the phone to his ear.

He starts to say something, but then speaks into the phone.

"Chinda. I'm sorry. I haven't had my phone with me. What happened? Are you at the hospital? Calm down and talk to me slowly."

Concerned, I move closer, trying to catch his sister's words. She's crying.

"I'll be there as soon as I can, but it's going to take a few hours," Rama tells her, and I get up and begin packing our things. "Is anybody there with you? Uncle Pavel? Can I talk to him? All right. I'll see you soon."

"Is it your father?" I ask when Rama disconnects.

The look he gives me is full of worry. "Pah had a heart attack. Chinda says she found him in his office, collapsed over the desk. Pete's dad's with her now, talking to the doctors."

We're in the car on our way home in less than twenty minutes.

Rama's quiet, and I'm worried about him. But the only thing I can do is get him to his sister and father as quickly and safely as possible.

CHAPTER TWENTY-TWO: Rama

When I walk into the hospital waiting room, my sister throws herself into my arms.

"Has something happened?" I ask, pushing her back so I can look at her tear-streaked face. "Is Pah..."

She shakes her head. "I'm just scared."

Relieved, I hug her. Behind me, Pravat rests a comforting hand on my shoulder.

My Uncle Pavel walks in. He's a shorter, broader version of my father with quite a bit more gray in his hair. Right now, his face is drawn and tired.

"Rama," he says, patting me on the back.

"How's Pah?" I ask.

"He's doing better. The procedure to remove the blockage went well. They're putting him in a private room now."

I release the breath I've been holding. "That's good."

"But there's some damage to the heart, and the doctors are saying he can't continue working as he has been. He's going to have to delegate to others."

"He's not going to want to do that," I say.

"No, he's not," Uncle Pavel agrees.

"Can I see him?" I ask.

My uncle nods.

"Will you stay with Chinda?" I ask Pravat.

"Of course."

I follow my uncle down the hall to a room. My first glimpse of my father is frightening. He's pale and seems smaller in the hospital bed with all the machines hooked to him. But he manages a smile when he sees me.

"Rama," he says. "I'm sorry you had to come back early."

"We were coming back in the morning anyway," I say, pulling a chair close to the bed. "Don't worry, Uncle Pavel and I will take care of everything."

"You're a good son," Pah says, closing his eyes. "I'm sorry. I'm just really tired."

"Sleep. It's good for you."

"Call Phichit. Explain what's happened, will you?"

"Of course. Don't worry about anything. I'm sure P'Phichit will be able to handle everything at the company."

When my father falls asleep, I get up from the chair and go to my uncle where he stands by the door.

"I'll stay here with him if you want to go home, Uncle Pavel. You look tired."

"I think I will now that he's out of the woods. I'll be back in the morning. Your Uncle Tin will be coming by, too."

I nod and walk into the hall to call the vice-president of my father's company, Phichit Kongkaeo. After I finish apprising him of the situation, I go back to the waiting room where Pravat is sitting with Chinda. He has her hand in his and is talking quietly to her while she cries into a wad of tissues. When she sees me, she jumps up.

"How is he? How does he look?"

"He's doing well," I tell her. "I spoke with him for a few minutes and he's resting now. I'm going to stay the night here with him. Can you call one of your friends and arrange to spend the night with them, so you don't have to be home alone?"

"I'm not leaving," Chinda says fiercely. "What if something happens and I'm not here?" I can see in her face she's thinking about our mother, and I relent.

"Okay."

"What can I do for you?" Pravat asks.

"If you could bring in my overnight bag, that would be great. I have an extra set of clothes in there and my toiletries. I should also have a T-shirt for Chinda to sleep in."

"Sure. I'll be right back."

After he leaves the room, I turn to Chinda. "They've cleared the blockage in Pah's heart. I promise, he's going to be fine."

Fresh tears slide down my sister's cheeks. "But what if it happens again?"

"We'll make sure it doesn't. He'll be put on medication, and he's going to have to stop working so hard."

"He'll never agree to that!" Chinda says.

Putting my arm around her shoulders, I pull her close. "He will. I've already talked to Khun Kongkaeo. He'll look after things at the company."

Chinda nods and blows her nose. "I didn't know what to do. He looked d-dead when I found him. I called for an ambulance. Then I called Uncle Pavel. He took care of everything here."

"You did everything right. You saved his life," I tell her, rubbing her arm. When the door opens, I look up, expecting to see Pravat, but it's one of my cousins. I give him an update, and when Pravat returns with my things, I talk to the nurse about the two of us sleeping in Pah's room.

"Thank you," I tell Pravat. "Please go home and get some rest. We're all right here."

He hesitates.

"Really," I say. "I'm going to make Chinda change and lie down. There's a couch and a recliner in the room we can sleep on."

"I'll bring you some breakfast in the morning before class," Pravat says.

"You don't have to."

"I want to," he says, squeezing my arm.

I watch him go, wishing I could spend tonight in his arms like I have the past several nights.

When Chinda sees our father, now sleeping, she bursts into tears again.

"He looks awful!" she whispers to me.

"He's been through a lot. He'll look better tomorrow. Go in the bathroom and change into this." I hand her one of the promotional T-shirts for season 2. The nurse comes in with some blankets and pillows, and I make our beds, giving Chinda the more comfortable-looking couch and taking the vinyl recliner for myself. When she returns from the bathroom, changed and face washed, I tuck her in before going into the bathroom and changing into a pair of sleep pants and another T-shirt.

IN LOVE

Chinda's already asleep when I turn out the lights. Stretching out on the recliner, I listen to the machines beeping and the quiet steps of the nurses outside the room. Several times during the night, someone comes in to check on Pah. I can't sleep. Now that everything has been taken care of, I'm shaky and uncertain. After spending a week sleeping in Pravat's arms, it feels empty and lonely not having him beside me.

Fortunately, Chinda sleeps soundly.

・♥・♥・♥・♥・♥・

I awaken when a nurse comes in to take my father's vital signs. Sitting up, I look out the window to see the sun peeking over the horizon. My eyes feel like they have sand in them, and I rub them, nodding to the nurse when she leaves. Chinda's still asleep. I know from experience that nothing short of an explosion will wake her up.

After using the bathroom, I return to the room to find Pravat there with three bags of food.

"How are you doing?" he asks softly, so as not to wake Pah or Chinda.

"Okay. I didn't sleep well, I'm afraid. That chair feels like it has rocks for stuffing." I rub at the small of my back.

"Looks like Chinda's sleeping okay," he says, looking to where my sister lies on the couch, dead to the world.

"Yeah. I'm glad. She was really upset last night. It really scared her finding him that way. I hate it that she had to deal with all that herself."

"She's strong like her big brother." Pravat says, placing the bags on a table. "I brought a little of everything. Enough for you guys and your uncles if they come early."

"Thank you so much," I tell him. Unable to help myself, I wrap my arms around him.

"Are you sure you're okay?" he asks.

"I am now that I've seen you."

His grip around me tightens. "I wish I could stay."

"It's okay." I let him go. "I know you have a class. Besides, I'm sure a lot of family will be by today."

"I'll come back this evening," Pravat promises.

"You don't have to."

"Rama." Prava's tone tells me not to argue.

"Okay. But don't push yourself. You can always call me."

Pravat looks over his shoulder at the door before pressing a kiss to my lips. "See you later. Be sure to eat."

I have three messages on my phone from my agent. Stepping outside the room, I dial Ace's number and listen to it ring four times before he picks up. Immediately, he starts in on me.

"Rama, you have got to be insane! Why did you sign up with all these ad agencies?"

"I didn't realize I should have only picked one or two," I say, running my hand through my hair. "Listen, I know I've gotten myself into a mess, but I need a couple of weeks. My father's had a heart attack."

Ace backs down a little when he hears that and promises he'll win me some time with the ad agencies. "But after that, you're going to be one busy guy," he warns me.

My cousin Sarah, Aunt Suzanne, and Uncle Pavel arrive an hour later. Chinda has awakened and sits cross-legged on the couch, eating some rice congee with pork that Pravat brought. She seems happy to see Sarah, who settles next to her on the couch.

My aunt and uncle have brought flowers and some books for Pah to read.

"Who brought this food?" Aunt Suzanne asks, looking through the bags.

"My friend Pravat dropped it off before he had to go to class."

"How considerate of him." Aunt Suzanne pulls a juice box out of the bag and inserts the straw.

"Has the doctor made his rounds yet?" Uncle Pavel asks.

"No, not yet. Pah's been sleeping since last night."

"I talked to Pete. He said to tell you he's thinking about you," Aunt Suzanne says. "I'm sure he'll call you soon." She smiles. "Pavel and I watched the first season of your series last week. I must say, you're very talented."

"Wait. That was your co-star here last night, wasn't it?" my uncle asks.

"Yes. Pravat Benjawan."

"Were you working when you found out about your father?"

"No, we were on vacation."

"Your Uncle Bank will be here this afternoon after his appointment," my aunt says just as Uncle Tin walks in. The oldest son, he's always felt like it's his job to take care of everyone in the family. It drives my father nuts.

"I hear Korn's doing better," Uncle Tin says quietly, looking to the bed where Pah peacefully sleeps before turning to me. "Hello, Rama."

"Hello, Uncle Tin." I give him the wai.

"Did you know your Aunt Sunnee is here?"

My heart seizes. "At the hospital?" I manage to ask.

"No, she's staying at my house. Pavel told me not to bring her. I have to say, she wasn't happy about it."

I close my eyes, relieved.

"Look," Uncle Tin says. "I don't know what happened between you and your aunt, but considering your father's condition and the wedding coming up, don't you think it's best to put your differences aside? It's hardly fair to keep her from her brother's hospital bed."

"Korn wouldn't want her here," Uncle Pavel says.

"He may have been angry at first, but—"

"She isn't welcome here." The voice coming from the bed is weak but adamant, and we all turn around to look at my father, who stares at his older brother with narrowed eyes.

"Korn," Tin says.

"Did you hear what I said? Tell Sunnee she's not welcome here."

"Now, Korn. Don't be hasty," Uncle Tin approaches the bed. "Sunnee's very worried about you and wants to see you. She arrived a few days ago and all she can talk about is making things right with you."

"She can't make this right! She hurt my son!" my father yells, startling all of us.

My aunt crosses the room and lays a hand on his shoulder. "All right, Korn. If that's what you want. We won't allow Sunnee to come. Calm down. You've been through a lot."

My father sinks back onto his pillow just before a nurse walks in and orders us all out. "The patient needs his rest."

CHAPTER TWENTY-THREE: Pravat

♥

It's dark by the time I pull into the hospital parking lot, and I'm tired. Now that final exams are approaching, all of my classes have ramped up the workload. I didn't sleep well the night before worrying about Rama, although this morning when I took breakfast to the hospital, he looked much better. I know he'll understand if I decide to go straight home, but I really want to see him.

When I step off the elevator, he's sitting in the waiting room looking pale and shaken. I'm immediately glad I came.

"Hey," I say, approaching him. "What's wrong?"

Rama almost knocks me off my feet when he jumps up and throws his arms around my neck. Wrapping him in a tight embrace, I whisper, "Hey, you're shaking. Is your father okay?"

Rama nods against my shoulder. "Just...don't let go of me a minute. Please?"

"Of course." I continue to hold him, even after his uncle who was there the night before walks into the room.

When Rama finally loosens his hold on me, he looks away. "I really needed that. Thanks."

"You don't have to thank me. I'll hold you any time you want me to."

His uncle's taken a seat on the other side of the room and is scrolling through his phone, not paying attention to us. "Have you eaten dinner?" I ask Rama.

He shakes his head. "I haven't had anything since breakfast, but my aunt and Uncle Tin have gone down the street to get some sandwiches. I'm really not hungry, though."

"Let's go down to the cafeteria. You need to get away for a minute. Do you want to look in on your father before we go?"

Rama shakes his head. "I was just in there. Uncle Bank's with him now. We can only go in one at a time now because my father got upset earlier."

"Where's Chinda?"

"Our cousin Sarah's taken her home to shower and change clothes."

When we reach the cafeteria, I coax Rama into eating a salad, and we sit down in one of the booths.

"Today's been rough, huh?" I ask, watching him poke at the quivering red dessert. "Why did your father get upset?"

"Uncle Tin brought up Aunt Sunnee. She's visiting him, and she wants to come see Pah."

"I'm sorry," I say. "That must have been hard on you."

"Uncle Tin acted like I was being selfish for not wanting her here. That's when Pah yelled at him. I had to leave the room and call my therapist."

"Did it help?"

Rama nods. "Have you ever been in therapy?" he asks curiously.

"Yeah. For a while, after the fire. It helped a lot."

"Why did you stop? Was it because you didn't need it anymore?"

"No, I just got busy. I've thought about going back because I still have disturbing dreams, though. Here." I take a spoon and scoop some of the gelatin up and hold it to his mouth. "Please eat, Rama," I say softly.

He parts his lips, and I slip the spoon between them. "Thank you."

"I know Uncle Tin doesn't believe me," he says after he swallows.

Hurting for him, I cover his hand with mine. "*I* believe you," I say. "And so do your father and sister. I'm sure there are others, too."

"I was so scared when I thought she had come to the hospital with Uncle Tin. I can't handle seeing her, and that makes me wonder how I'm going to get through the wedding."

"You could always not go," I tell him. "Why put yourself through that?"

Rama shakes his head. I hope he at least considers it. I convince him to finish the salad, and when we head back upstairs, I think he looks a little stronger. As soon as we enter the waiting room, Rama's Uncle Pavel says, "Korn is asking for you, Rama."

"Go home and get some rest. I'll be fine," Rama tells me.

Nodding, I watch him walk down the hall and enter his father's room before I turn to walk toward the elevators.

When I round the corner, an older man steps into my path. As he looks quite a bit like Korn and Pavel, I assume it's Rama's Uncle Tin.

"You're the guy who played in that series with Rama," he says.

"Yes, Uncle." I give the wai and introduce myself.

Tin gives me a once over. "Where's Rama?"

"He just ate and is visiting his father now. Excuse me, Uncle. I need to get home."

He steps back to let me pass, and I feel his eyes on me until I step on the elevator.

Back at my apartment, I send Rama a quick text, "SuSu," to encourage him to stay strong before settling into bed and checking social media. The first episode of season two aired tonight and "Pravma" shippers are in full force, commenting that Lin and I were never a couple. I'm glad the sham is over. Our fans have adopted the grumpy face emoji for Rama, and the rainbow for me. I think the latter came from the support that poured out toward me after Preed said I was gay. Even those who don't believe it's true use the rainbow emoji for me now. Tons of grumpy faces and rainbows dot the comment section, along with hearts of all colors.

The support of our fans makes me smile. Plugging my phone to the charger, I settle down to sleep.

CHAPTER TWENTY-FOUR: Rama

A week and a half has passed. My father is home, and Chinda and I walk on eggshells around him because he's frustrated at not being allowed to take an early morning run and then spend fifteen hours at the office like he's accustomed to doing.

On the second day Pah is home, Aunt Sunnee calls me. I don't answer, but she leaves a voicemail that I spend two days staring at in my notifications until I finally get up the nerve to listen to it.

"Rama, I want to see my brother. I'm worried about him. I want you to think about how, by fabricating this story and pulling our family apart, you've contributed to the state he's in right now. Shame on you! You've got to tell the truth."

My hands shake as I delete the message. I hate myself for the shame and doubt that creep over me after hearing her words. I know what happened, but part of me keeps thinking, *How can she be so bold? Could she somehow be right, and I made it all up in my head? Did the death of my mother mess me up that much?*

Pravat has been busy with school, and although we talk every day, I don't get to see him, other than a couple of quick lunches. I don't want to burden him with my problems and make him worry when he has a full plate, so I've kept our conversations light. We have hired a home nurse, which has reduced my stress enough that I can make appearances and shoot commercials for the ad agencies with whom I signed contracts.

Uncle Pavel suggests a family meeting to discuss how Pah needs to change his lifestyle. The idea breaks me into a cold sweat because I don't know if my Uncle Tin will bring Aunt Sunnee. I know Uncle Pavel is on my side, and I just have to trust he'll prevent that from happening.

I'm surprised when I get a call from Two asking me to meet him for lunch at a local restaurant. The first thing that pops into my mind is that Mint has urged him to ask me if Pravat and I are keeping quiet about them. It turns out I'm not off the mark. After I assure Two that Pravat and I have no interest in exposing them, he sighs.

"I like him, Rama. I know he's a dick, but I like him. And he's really not that bad when he lets you get to know him. It took a long time for him to let me in. We were having so many arguments at first that P'Tida made us go on a weekend retreat together, remember?"

I nod.

"Things changed after that. We got close that weekend. Not physically—that came later. But now, since the beach, Mint won't have anything to do with me. He cut the trip short and only called me the other day because he wanted to know if we could trust you and Pravat not to tell anyone. I told him we could, but he's so worried, I promised

I'd talk to you." He gives me a sheepish smile. "And I guess I needed someone to talk to."

"I'm really sorry." I don't know what else to say. I don't think Mint is going to turn into Two's Prince Charming.

Two nods. "It is what it is. So, you and Pravat? I kind of guessed. There was no way he was into Lin. That was P'Tida's idea, huh?"

I could try to deny that there's anything between me and Pravat except friendship, but Two can hardly rat on us when we have the same information about him. "Yeah. It's been difficult for us. I'm sure you understand why."

Two nods and finally tackles the burger he ordered.

"You want to be together but still maintain your careers," he says after swallowing, reaching for his drink. "But you're so popular as a couple. If you're going to remain one on screen, does it matter if you're the same off?"

"I've been thinking about that. I don't think fans will like us as much if they know we're really a couple. It takes away the excitement and mystery. Some of them were even happy thinking Pravat's with Lin." I pause, thinking. "I would be okay if I can't act in bl dramas, but I don't want to ruin Pravat's career."

We change the subject after that, and by the time we part, I'm happy to see Two is a little brighter than he was when we met in front of the restaurant.

When I return home, several cars are in the driveway. I call Chinda. "Who's here?"

"Who's where? I'm at the store."

I sigh. "There are several cars at the house, and I don't recognize any of them except Uncle Tin's. Hurry home."

Promising myself if Aunt Sunnee is there I will turn around and leave, I walk inside. Uncle Tin sits on the couch, talking with my father, who looks tired. In the corner, the nurse sits with a pile of knitting on his lap.

I greet my uncle before asking my father, "Do you want to take a nap?"

"What am I, five?" he scoffs.

"Have you had lunch?" I told Chinda to prepare something for him, but she might have forgotten.

"Yes, yes," he says irritably. He's never liked to be fussed over.

"You been out with your boyfriend?" Uncle Tin asks with a scowl.

"That's Rama's business," Pah says sharply. "Mind your own."

"Pavel's kid is marrying another man, and now Rama is dating one? What will people say? Pretty soon everyone's going to be talking about our family, and that *is* my business," my uncle argues.

My heart's pounding in my ears. I sit down, and concentrate on my breathing as my uncle continues, "I can hear it now. Rama Sathianthai, son of an important Bangkok businessman, is making sissy television shows, dating a man, and accusing his family of molesting him. It'll be all over the news. Next thing you know, we'll have investors pulling out."

"*We'll?*" my father asks coldly. "Do I need to remind you that you've never been interested in the family business? Our father appointed me CEO, not you."

"That doesn't mean I want to see everything our father worked for turn to dust because you can't handle your son!" my uncle shouts.

"Tin," my Uncle Pavel says from the doorway. I hadn't even heard him and Aunt Suzanne arrive. "Perhaps you better leave. You're upsetting Korn."

Behind him Chinda stands holding two bags of groceries, her face white. Aunt Suzanne takes the two bags from her and leads her into the kitchen.

"I agree that it's in my patient's best interest if you leave," the nurse says to Uncle Tin. He's big and burly, and although my Uncle Tin looks like he wants to argue, he doesn't. Uncle Pavel walks him out.

"I'm sorry," I begin, but my father cuts me off.

"Tin is an ass. Don't pay attention to a word he says."

I'm not sure what to make of this. Pah hasn't been pleased that I'm seeing Pravat, but he's defending me anyway.

"But your company..." I trail off.

"Nobody gives a shit if my son is gay or not," Pah snaps. "As for the other thing, Tin is going to have to accept what Sunnee did."

Stunned, I can only nod before hurrying to the kitchen to help Chinda and Aunt Suzanne.

CHAPTER TWENTY-FIVE: Pravat

It's the old nightmare. I come home from work to find the house in flames and three fire trucks parked in front of our house, their revolving lights eerily flashing over the faces of a dozen or so neighbors. Firemen hold me back, preventing me from running into the flames to save my mother and brothers. I vomit into the ditch while the hand of a stranger gently pats my back. The dream is always a combination of memories and terrible things my mind makes up to torment me in my sleep.

Waking in a cold sweat, I rush to the bathroom to void what little is in my stomach before getting ready for school.

Most of my courses during my final semester are electives I've chosen to round out my credits, such as Theater in Education, that I find tedious and uninteresting. Except for one. I'm surprisingly enjoying my film directing class. Directing isn't something I ever thought I'd want to do, but this class has ignited an interest in me that has got me thinking about pursuing it in the future. It's late afternoon and I'm drained. But canceling dinner with Rama never occurs to me. I need to be there for him. His cousin's wedding is two weeks away, and with his impossible schedule lately, we have to see each other when we can.

My head pounds underneath the spray of the shower as I wash away the day. I swallow a few pain relievers for the headache that's been with me all day before throwing on a fresh set of clothes and rushing out of my apartment to meet Rama.

When I enter the hotel where the restaurant is located, I smooth back my hair and straighten my collar before walking through the door and looking around. It doesn't take me long to spot Rama at the far end of the room, as he's easily the handsomest man in the room. He also looks untouchable, which is fine with me. When he sees me, he flashes a gorgeous smile that melts me from the inside out.

"Have you been waiting long?" I ask him as I sit down.

"Only a few minutes," he assures me. "How was your day?"

His eyes look tired, and stress lines mar his forehead. I'm not about to dump my problems on him.

"Great. Everything's wrapping up. How about you?"

Rama nods. "Good. I had to do some finagling to be able to free up the date of Pete's wedding."

The waiter appears to take our drink order, and when he leaves, Rama says quietly, "I'm dreading it so much, Pravat."

"I know." Under cover of the table, I brush my calf against his, and his face relaxes slightly. A moment later, I'm surprised to feel his stockinged foot edge under the cuff of my pant leg. Gazes locked, we sip our drinks in silence. We haven't come together physically since the beach, and I want him badly. The flush working its way up Rama's neck tells me he feels the same. My gaze follows his tongue as it swipes his full lower lip. I'm seized with a longing so strong it takes my breath away.

The waiter returns, and I clear my throat, pulling my mind back from where it was going. We order from the menu, and when we're alone again, I smile at Rama.

"Can I stay with you tonight?" he suddenly asks.

"Of course," I say. "You have time?"

He nods. "My first appointment isn't until eleven, and, if I remember right, you have a late class on Wednesdays." He smiles slyly. "I brought my overnight bag, just in case."

I'm going to have a difficult time getting through dinner in the state he's put me in.

Rama tells me about his father's recent change of heart concerning us.

"That's wonderful. It must be a load off your mind, too."

He nods. "It really is. Knowing Pah is okay with us means a lot."

The food arrives and we eat, but there's an underlying charge in our conversation as we anticipate going home together. I'm glad I made the bed and straightened up this morning before leaving for school, although I'm pretty sure I dropped my towel from the shower and the day's clothes in a heap on the floor before heading for the restaurant.

When we leave, Rama follows me in his car to my building, and the entire drive, my mind's full of all the things I want to do to him. By the time we park our cars, I'm so hot and bothered, I can't get him alone fast enough. Taking his hand, I tug him into the building, past the guard and into the elevator, pressing him against the wall as soon as the doors close on us and kissing him hard.

"Pravat," he gasps out when the elevator doors slide open, then lets out a surprised cry when I lift him off his feet and carry him down the hall to my door.

"What if someone comes out of their apartment?" he hisses at me, face scarlet.

I have to set him down in order to unlock my door, but as soon as we're inside and I see his mouth that I've kissed into a red, ripe strawberry, my hunger intensifies, and I'm on him again. This time, I attack the long, sweet-smelling column of his neck, marking its paleness with my teeth as I go.

He groans, long and loud.

"It's been too long," I say before biting the soft skin underneath his ear.

Rama tugs my shirt from inside the waistband of my slacks and slides his hands underneath, running cool fingers up my abdomen to find my nipples, and I exhale loudly from my nose in the middle of a fiery kiss as he tweaks them.

"What do you want, sweetheart?" I ask. He trembles in my arms at the endearment, the first I've ever used with him.

Breathing picking up, he keens as I nibble his collarbone.

"Bed," he manages to say.

For the second time, I lift him off his feet, this time carrying him across the apartment to pin him to the mattress. His soft grunts and groans as we explore each other's mouths drive me crazy, and I don't lose any time unbuttoning his shirt and getting his pants open. Rama is just as busy tugging off my clothes, and when our mouths meet again, I nearly lose my breath at the feel of skin-to-skin contact.

"Want you," Rama says. "All of you. Now. Please, Pravat."

With a loud groan, I divest him of his pants and underwear and throw them across the room, uncaring where they land. I can't believe I worried earlier about the cleanliness of the apartment—in the state he's in, Rama isn't going to notice, and we're about to mess things up a lot more. I take his hot shaft in my palm and attack his neck again with my mouth.

Rama arches into me, his cries getting louder in the quiet room.

"I'm not going to last long," I say unsteadily, stroking him with confident twists of my hand.

"Inside me. Please! I need it."

Fuck, his begging makes me lose the little bit of control I have left.

I reach for the lube, nearly spilling the contents of the bedside drawer in the process. In my fevered excitement, I somehow manage to ready myself before lifting Rama's legs and pushing into him without finesse or care, the sight of the love bites I've left all over his neck and chest driving me to distraction.

The cords of his neck straining, Rama arches beneath me, tight heat massaging me with every powerful thrust of my cock. Face awash with pleasure, he wraps his legs around my waist, pulling me deeper into the hot clutch of his body, fingernails scratching a searing path down my bare back before clutching my ass.

At the edge of sanity, I spear into him again and again, chasing the tease of my orgasm while his cries grow more and more desperate.

I fuck him hard and fast, every other thrust ending in a delicious grind, until I explode, barely cognizant enough to bring him with me with a few strokes of my hand.

· ❤ · ❤ · ❤ · ❤ · ❤ ·

"Pravat."

I awake to Rama softly calling my name, his fingers stroking my hair. It takes several seconds to pull me out of the horror of the dream. This time it was so vivid, I swear I could feel the flames licking at my skin.

My eyes flutter open as soft lips press to my temple.

"Are you okay?"

I nod, swallowing thickly before reaching for the bottle of water I keep at my bedside and taking a long drink. Outside the window, the river is peaceful in the moonlight. I offer Rama the bottle and he takes a sip before screwing the top back on and placing it back on the nightstand.

"That must have been one hell of a bad dream," he says when we're settled in each other's arms.

"An old nightmare of the night of the fire. I've been having it a lot lately."

Lifting his head, Rama says, "I'm sorry."

I pull him in for a kiss before settling his head on my shoulder again, my fingers burrowing into his soft, thick hair.

"It's the stress of exams. I'll stop having it soon."

"Have you thought any more about getting back into therapy?" Rama asks.

I really should. These dreams are proof there are things I need to talk out. "I'll make an appointment," I promise. Running my free hand over the contours of his smooth back, my thoughts turn to our earlier activities. "How do you feel? Was I too rough?"

"I liked it," Rama says against my skin, and damn if my cock doesn't react to that statement. It gives another jerk when Rama raises his head and runs his tongue over my left nipple.

"You're stepping into dangerous territory," I warn him, cock growing hard and hot against his leg. Rama answers by reaching for the lube, squirting a liberal amount on his hand, and flipping back the covers to run slick fingers over me. I close my eyes and moan, but my eyes fly back open when Rama straddles me and lowers himself onto my erection. For the next fifteen minutes, he rides me with slow, tortuous twists of his hips until I'm nearly out of my mind. When I finally come, my fingerprints are all over his pale hips and long, white ropes of his cum paint my torso.

"Holy shit," I mutter when he collapses on top of me. I can't keep myself from reaching between his round cheeks and touching the place where we're attached.

"Dirty boy," he teases, and I slap his rump just to hear him gasp. Lifting his head, he looks at me wide-eyed.

I grin. "Who's the dirty boy? I'm pretty sure you're the one who just mounted me and took me for a ride."

"Pretty sure, huh?" Rama mumbles, his cheeks reddening as he ducks his head. I kiss his temple, and we settle down to recover.

The next thing I know, Rama's phone alarm is going off.

"Shit," he says, glancing at the time. Sitting up, he rubs his eyes. "I have to be across town in forty-five minutes."

"No time for breakfast?" I ask, pouting a little.

"I'm afraid not."

Watching him cross the room naked and disappear into the bathroom, I stretch on the bed. My body feels spent and sore, as though I've spent a couple hours at the gym. I can only imagine how Rama's ass must feel. I'm a little embarrassed at how aggressive I was last night, but by the way he just rode me, I think he's okay.

"Down boy," I say to my stirring cock. "That'll have to suffice for a while."

Rama comes out of the bathroom dressed, and, shoving his toiletries into his bag, he zips it up and puts it over his shoulder before regarding me still lying in bed.

"Aren't you lucky, getting to lie around for another hour."

"I'm not the one who signed up with seven ad agencies," I remind him.

"Wipe that smirk off your face. Call me tonight." He heads for the door.

"It might be late," I call to him.

"I don't care."

CHAPTER TWENTY-SIX: Rama

♥

When my father walks into my bedroom, I quickly whip out the pillow I've tucked under me and throw it onto the bed, wincing when my ass hits the chair. I don't want him to wonder why I'm using it. I've been sore all day. I had to make up a story about falling on my ass to the shampoo company to explain why I was sitting so gingerly.

"Pah, what are you doing up so late?" I ask because it's well after midnight. I haven't been home long and just got off a video call with Pravat.

Pah sits on the edge of my bed. He's wearing his navy- blue silk pajamas with the red edging and looks well-rested for the first time in a long time.

"I've gotten into the habit of napping in the afternoon. My sleep schedule is completely off." He sighs. "I'm bored staying at home all day. Tomorrow my secretary is bringing me some files."

"Pah, please be careful. Don't undo all you've done for your recovery."

"I won't. I've discussed this with my doctor, and he's approved light work for the next couple of weeks."

I look at him dubiously. "I wonder if you'll stick to just light work, though."

"I will. Believe me, I don't want to have another heart attack." He sighs again. "Your poor sister. I wish she hadn't been the one to have to find me."

Immediately, I feel guilty. "I should have been here."

"It's not your fault. You have a life to live and can't be here all the time. If anyone's to blame, it's me for not taking care of myself better. I thought because I exercised and ate reasonably, all the stress and late hours wouldn't matter. I was wrong."

My father rarely admits he's wrong. Not because he's egotistical, but because he gives everything he does careful thought before acting on it. I've tried to emulate him but haven't been very successful at it, as I tend to be impulsive.

"Rama." He waits until I meet his eyes. "I meant what I said before. I accept your relationship with Pravat."

Wide-eyed, I can only stare.

"If you say you love him, then you must. I don't want us to be in opposition over it. Are you planning on inviting him to Pete's wedding?"

"Do you think that will be all right?" I ask. Having Pravat there with me would be extremely comforting.

"I think you should do exactly as you want to do. Chinda and I will support you."

"Uncle Tin—"

"Don't worry about your Uncle Tin," my father says definitively.

"Have you talked to Aunt Sunnee?" I ask. I need to know.

"Briefly."

"Did she tell you I'm lying?"

"I know you aren't lying, Son." He stands.

My nose stings, and I'm suddenly afraid I'm going to burst into tears in front of my father.

"I'm heading to bed now. Sleep well."

· ♥ · ♥ · ♥ · ♥ · ♥ ·

A week later, my sister goes to Sarah's to spend the night, and my father decides to leave the house for the first time since being released from the hospital and to go the movies with Bank. Uncle Bank's health continues to deteriorate, and I know Pah wants to spend more time with him. Before leaving, he suggests I invite Pravat over for a swim.

After an hour of horsing around in the water, we rest against the side of the pool.

"Would you be willing to attend Pete and Alex's wedding with me?" I ask Pravat.

"Of course. If that's what you want." Hovering close to my face long enough for butterflies to take off in my chest, he presses a sweet, lingering kiss to my mouth.

"If we were in a bl drama, we would be doing this underwater," I tease when we part.

Chuckling, Pravat shakes his head, rubbing our noses together before leaning back against the side of the pool. "I had one of those scenes in my last drama. It was so difficult to film. Holding your breath, trying to remain submerged when your body wants to float to the surface, trying to look like you're enjoying a kiss when you really just want to suck in some air."

I laugh with him. "Sounds awful." I raise my brows. "Want to try it?"

Together, we take deep breaths and sink under, flapping our arms to get closer to each other once submerged. With a little effort, our mouths come together, bubbles escaping our noses. Imagining a cameraman in a diving suit nearby, I want to laugh. In the end, I have to rise to the surface or drown.

"How many takes?" I ask when Pravat joins me.

He wrinkles his brow. "Ah, I think at least ten."

"And this was with Preed?"

He nods, making a face. "It was ten times worse doing it with him."

Pravat tugs me until our chests touch and kisses me again, this time parting his lips and deepening it. With every soft brush of his tongue, I slip a little more into a daze.

As darkness descends, the soft lights inside the pool activate, casting a warm glow over the two of us entwined in the water. Pravat picks me up, and I wind my legs wind around his waist. All around us, there's nothing but the sound of night bugs, water dripping, and our fevered moans as we try to consume each other with our hands, lips, and teeth.

"Ah!" Pravat's teeth skim across my neck. Between us, our erections try to burn their way through the material of our bathing suits.

"Can't wait," I answer, shoving my bathing suit down and off my legs. Somewhere between our first time and now, I've evidently become shameless.

Another hot kiss, and then Pravat's pushing inside me. It hurts, and I dig my fingers into his shoulders, but we don't break our kiss and pretty soon he's buried all the way inside me and the searing pain is turning into something much more enjoyable.

"Rama," Pravat says on a moan before withdrawing almost all the way and plunging back in.

My cry is quickly swallowed by Pravat's mouth, and, lost in his kiss, I begin to relax. His deep thrusts are hitting in just the right place, and it isn't long before I'm so turned on, I can't do anything but moan into his neck and hang on. Soon, though, we both become frustrated by the way water is slowing us down, and he withdraws from my body.

"This isn't working," he says. "You're bedroom?"

"I won't be able to hear when Pah returns from there," I say. Desperate to have him back inside me, I suggest a lawn chair.

"Devil," he whispers with a naughty wink before kissing me deeply.

That's when I hear the garage door, and it's a scramble for us to get our shorts back in place and try to look innocent.

CHAPTER TWENTY-SEVEN: Rama

♥

I look around at the crowd of students in front of the Faculty of Arts building until I spot Pravat sitting at a table. It hasn't been long since I graduated, but already I feel a million miles away from these people.

I stride across the grass, hesitating only a brief moment before walking up to the table. He flashes me a smile when he sees me, and my heart jumps in my chest.

"Rama." Making room on the bench for me to sit, he then turns to his three friends. "Everyone, this is Rama Sathianthai."

"Oh, we all know who he is," a slim boy sitting across from Pravat says cheerfully. "I'm Bass." He points to the smaller boy next to him who's holding a fizzy orange drink, and then to a pretty girl with glasses. "This is Spin and Cushion."

"Sawasdee khrap, Nongs," I say, giving the wai.

Spin grins at me, returning the gesture before wrapping his lips back around the straw of his drink. He has to be college age, but he looks much younger.

"We're all in dramatic arts. Well, except for Kiet. He's in Engineering but comes over to eat with us every day," Bass says.

I smile at Kiet, who gives me a friendly nod over his bowl of noodles. His dark hair is streaked with purple.

Pravat wraps his arm around my shoulders because we've decided that we're going to gradually come out as a couple, and Pravat's friends are the first to know.

Pravat meets my eyes, and a soft, squishy feeling overtakes me as he says, "Rama's my boyfriend."

"Really?" Cushion turns to Pravat with wide eyes behind her glasses. "Wow! When did this happen? During filming?"

"It's developed slowly," Pravat says.

I feel a blush climbing up my neck.

"It's about time you two made it official," Kiet says around a mouthful of noodles. "I knew it would happen, though."

Pravat elbows him in the side. "Could you swallow before you talk, buffalo?"

Leaning forward so I can see around Pravat, I look questioningly at Kiet. "How did you know?"

"I just had a feeling when Pravat told me about your audition."

"Kiet and his *feelings*," Bass teases.

"Yeah, he thinks he's psychic," Spin says, then glances at me shyly before sucking on his straw.

"No, I don't, Baby. I just have a second sense about things, that's all." Kiet shrugs.

Confused, I look at Kiet. Did he just call Spin *baby*? Because I know for a fact Kiet has a girlfriend.

Noticing, Cushion explains, "He means 'baby,' like, literally. We all call him that most of the time. It's because Spin's so cute. His face is like a baby's."

Spin rolls his eyes and pouts, but the pout turns into a grin when Cushion places some of her chicken on his plate at the same time that Bass gives him a couple of meatballs. It appears the group likes to coddle him.

"It's not just that he's cute," Bass reminds them. "He played Baby in a production of *Dirty Dancing* freshman year. Remember?"

"'Nobody puts Baby in a corner!'" Kiet quotes, and we all laugh.

"You played a girl's part?" I ask Spin.

"Our drama teacher is so cool. She rewrote the script to make it Thai, and she changed Baby into a boy so I could play the part," Spin tells me with a happy smile.

"That *is* cool. Who played Johnny?" I ask.

Spin turns pink and concentrates on his drink, but Bass turns and scans the tables around us. "Over there. The good-looking one with the smirk. They were on fire together. I'll show you a clip sometime. I have several on my phone."

"Don't you dare," Spin threatens, the tips of his ears turning a dark red. Taking pity on him, I change the subject, asking about their faculty and if they're ready for graduation.

When Kiet finishes eating, Pravat excuses himself to walk him partway back to Kiet's faculty building. When Bass and Cushion get into a conversation about an exam, Spin comes around the table to sit next to me.

"I want to ask you something," he says, looking at me with eyes as black and round as marbles. "How do you like playing in bl dramas?"

"Yeah, I enjoy it. Of course, I've only been in one. But I've been lucky enough to have a really good experience both seasons. Not everyone does."

He nods. "I know all about what that guy did to Pravat. I'm glad he got paired with you this time."

I can't help but stare. With his dark cap of wavy black hair, full lips dark as a cherry, and innocent eyes blinking up at me, I can easily see why his friends fawn over him.

"Do you want to act in bl's?" I ask him. If he's talented, he could likely get a part.

Spin nods. "I'm thinking about auditioning."

"Have you asked Pravat his opinion?"

"Yeah. He seemed wary, but all my friends are really protective of me like that." He scowls, and somehow that's cute, too.

"I think you should do what you want to do," I say. "Just go in with your eyes open, and don't automatically trust everyone. Pravat will mentor you. I will, too, if you'd like." I pity the guy who tries to take advantage of this boy because there will be a line of people waiting to give retribution.

Spin's grin is full of sparkling white teeth. "Thanks, Rama!"

Pravat returns, and I stand.

"I have to go," I say. "Nice to meet you, everyone."

There's a chorus from goodbyes from Pravat's friends, and Pravat walks me to my car.

"Was it okay that I told them today?" he asks.

"Of course. Your friends are nice. I like them."

"Yeah. I'm lucky to have such a great gang. Kiet's kind of an unofficial member, since he's in a different faculty and has a group he hangs with in Engineering, too. But he and I have known each other since high school."

We reach my car parked underneath some shady trees, and Pravat takes my hand, fiddling with my fingers like he's nervous.

"What is it?" I ask. "You aren't sorry you told them about us, are you?"

"What?" He looks at me in surprise. "No, not at all. I just don't want you to leave, that's all. I've been missing you."

I smile. "I miss you, too, but I have to go peddle skin products." The advertising promos are about to kill me. They're all I do.

"I know," he says before leaning in and kissing me. I return the kiss, although I'm a little embarrassed because, although we're alone, someone could walk over at any minute. But I want to kiss him more than I'm worried about that.

When we pull away, he tells me he'll talk to me later, and I watch him walk back across the grass to his friends before getting into my car.

CHAPTER TWENTY-EIGHT: Pravat

♥

Last night was the night before Pete and Alex's wedding, and he stayed with me at my apartment. I spent a lot of time trying to get him to relax, an endeavor that proved enjoyable for the both of us as the deep-tissue massage I gave him turned into a wild bout of sex. I have to say, Rama might have been nervous about having sex with a man, but once he tried it, he was all in. Due to our enthusiastic activities, we accidentally slept late the next morning and had to rush to get dressed so as not to be late for the ceremony.

"You look very handsome," I tell him as we stand in the parking area of the outdoor venue. Rama's navy-blue suit fits his lean form perfectly, and the pale pink shirt he wears with it complements his complexion.

"You do, too." He straightens the collar of my gray jacket. "I'm so nervous." He leans closer to me and whispers, "And my ass is sore."

I don't allow the swell of masculine pride that fills me at that statement to show because I don't want to tease Rama when he's in this state, but the thought of the love bites I left all over his body are enough to make me want to push him into the back seat of the car and...

"Pravat. What are you thinking about?" Rama asks coyly, and I feel myself blush.

Taking my hand, he begins walking toward where people are seating themselves on white folding chairs in front of an archway of flowers in the distance.

"Everything will be fine," I promise, squeezing his hand as we walk. His face has become serious, and I notice he's avoiding looking at the crowd.

"Alex's family attended the legal ceremony in the states, so I guess we can sit anywhere," he says when we reach the seating area.

"Let's sit here in the back so we can easily leave if you want to. Unless you want to sit with your dad and sister—I see them in the front row."

Rama shakes his head. "No. Here's good." We sit down. I feel a lot of eyes on us, and, as this wedding has two grooms, I don't think it's because we're holding hands.

"Is she here?" Rama whispers.

"What does she look like?"

"Tall and thin. She wears her hair up. At least, she used to." Taking his phone out of his pocket, he says, "I'll text Pah and tell him where we are."

I look around at the seats near the front. I recognize Pete's parents, Suzanne and Pavel, from the hospital. And next to them, Tin. On his right is an older woman with a sour expression. She keeps leaning in and talking to Tin, and every once in a while, her eyes scan the crowd. When they meet mine, I don't look away or even blink. Her eyes move from me to Rama, and I see them harden. Looking away, she moves around Tin, and across the aisle to Korn and Chinda.

"Is that her going to speak to your dad?" I ask Rama, although I feel pretty certain.

Rama's head comes up, and when he looks in that direction, his face pales. "Shit. She's going to upset Pah and cause a scene at Pete and Alex's wedding."

Lacing our fingers together, I squeeze his hand reassuringly. "Your Uncle Pavel isn't about to let that happen, especially at his son's wedding." I'm right; we watch as Pavel follows his sister and quietly says something to her, to which she angrily snaps back before talking to Korn again. When he turns away from her, refusing to speak, she finally walks away with Pavel and sits down again.

The ceremony begins, which consists of Pete and Alex saying their written vows to each other with their attendants standing with them. It isn't a traditional American or Thai wedding, but rather something they've put together to fit their situation. And it's nice. When everyone applauds, the couple invites those present to have refreshments under the tent.

"What do you want to do?" I ask Rama.

"I don't know," he says, then shakes his head. "All this time I was so insulted that Pete didn't ask me to stand up with him at his wedding. But the whole time they were saying their vows, all I could think of was how glad I wasn't up there with all those eyes on me. And I would have been standing right in front of *her*."

"Why don't we go home?" I suggest. "You can sign the guest book, and Pete will know you were here."

"I don't want to run. It isn't fair," Rama said.

"Let's go get some food then," I say, standing.

Straightening his shoulders, Rama leads me out of our row of seats to the left and we cross the grass to the large tent covering several tables of food.

"Rama, it's been such a long time," a woman greets him.

"Sawasdee khrap, Auntie," Rama says before introducing me as his boyfriend.

It takes me a minute to come back to myself after that. The woman doesn't seem to be particularly phased, but others standing nearby are staring and talking. The woman begins talking about Rama in his childhood, and I'm only listening with half an ear, more concerned that my lover's posture is becoming more and more stiff as the minutes tick by.

Wrapping my arm around his waist, I inch closer so that our bodies touch, doing my best to shelter him the only way I know how, and I'm rewarded when Rama relaxes a little bit. We talk to a few more people in a similar way before we make it over to Pete and Alex, who are surrounded by friends and family.

"Congratulations," Rama tells them both, exchanging hugs. His words and actions seem heart-felt, and I'm glad to know his hurt and animosity for his favorite cousin seem to be fading.

During this time, I somehow managed to forget about Rama's aunt, perhaps thinking she wouldn't dare to approach him at this event, although from what I've seen she seems to be bold.

Then a female voice behind us makes Rama flinch and his face go deathly pale.

CHAPTER TWENTY-NINE: Rama

♥

"Rama."

Just hearing my aunt saying my name makes me start shaking. I want to be stronger than this, but my body won't cooperate. Pravat's arm tightens around me, and, as the world tilts, I'm sure he's going to be holding me up any second if I have to face Aunt Sunnee. But my father's voice, loud and authoritative, saves me.

"Sunnee, I have told you to stay away from my son."

Alex and Pete look unsure of what to do as my father and his sister face off, and, despite the fact that I didn't want any of this, I feel guilty that it's all happening at their wedding celebration.

"We can't ignore this forever, Korn," Aunt Sunnee says defiantly. "You need to tell your boy to apologize to me for what he's done and set things to rights!"

Behind her, Uncle Pavel is pushing his way through the gathering crowd to get to us. He grabs his sister by the arm. "Sunnee, this is my son's special day, and I will not have you ruining it! If I have to drag you out of her kicking and screaming, I will do it."

"He's lied about me!" Sunnee yells, pointing at me. My eyes meet with hers, and the crazed look in them shocks me.

"Breathe," Pravat whispers in my ear. Slowly, I suck in air then let it out.

Turning away from Sunnee, I meet eyes with an older man nearby. I recognize him and his wife as old neighbors of Pete's family. At the moment, they look half-fascinated, half-appalled by the family drama spinning out in front of them. Pravat's hand wraps around my wrist, and he begins tugging me toward the front of the tent as my aunt continues to shout.

"He's said terrible, unconscionable things about me, and I want an apology! Korn! I demand you make him do it, do you hear me?"

As we hurry across the grass toward the parking lot, someone catches up to us.

"Are you all right, Rama?" It's my older cousin Mark, Uncle Bank's only son who now lives in Cambodia. He falls into step with us.

"P'Mark. Yes, I just need to get out of here. I shouldn't have come."

"No, Aunt Sunnee shouldn't have come," Mark says as we come to a stop beside Pravat's car.

"I couldn't agree more," Pravat says. I regret asking him to come with me because, although he's been my rock, what just happened was something he shouldn't have witnessed or experienced.

As I introduce him to Mark, my gaze remains fixed on the group under the tent where it looks as though Uncle Pavel is indeed dragging his sister away from the gathering. Sunnee flails, knocking over one of the tent poles, and it sags. Several people rush to keep it the canopy from falling on the nearest table of food.

I wince, repeating, "I shouldn't have come."

"It's her fault, not yours, Nong," Mark says, bringing my attention to him. "I've only heard about everything going on between you and Aunt Sunnee in the past few days. I'm sorry."

"You believe me?" I ask, unsure.

"Of course. And I told my father that."

"I don't think a lot of them agree with you."

Mark looks down at his feet. Across the lawn, loud exclamations follow when the tent collapses over the crowd's heads.

"I'd like to think I'd believe you regardless," Mark says, "but, unfortunately, Aunt Sunnee showed her true character to me, also, years ago."

"What?" I can't think. Is Mark saying that Aunt Sunnee...

"Can we go somewhere to talk? I can meet you guys somewhere." Mark asks, looking over his shoulder. I follow his gaze to see guest crawling out from under the tent while Aunt Sunnee continues to screech and claw at my uncle.

Pravat suggests a restaurant close by, and we climb into our cars.

"What do you think P'Mark meant by that?" I ask Pravat on the way.

"It sounds like your aunt did something similar to him. I wonder why he's only heard about everything recently."

"He's been working in Phnom Penh City for the past few years. He and his father have never seen eye-to-eye, but with Uncle Bank's health deteriorating, I suppose P'Mark wanted to mend fences," I say. I'm having a lot of trouble wrapping my mind around everything that has happened in the last twenty minutes. As we drive past the grounds,

I see that the venue's security has taken control of the situation, and guests are being escorted away from the fallen tent.

Once inside the restaurant, we settle into a booth in the back and order food.

"P'Mark, can you explain what you said about Aunt Sunnee?" I ask, unable to wait any longer.

Mark nods. "When I was seventeen, my family went to visit relatives in America. We stayed at a hotel near Aunt Sunnee and Uncle Roger's house, and one night, after she and Uncle Roger had dinner with us, they came up to our suite for drinks. I went to bed. Later, Aunt Sunnee came into my room and did something unexpected and shocking."

Underneath the table, Pravat rests his hand on my thigh.

"Did...did she touch you?" I ask.

Mark nods. "She stood talking to me for a few minutes. I could hear my parents and Uncle Roger chatting and laughing in the next room. Sunnee started casually smoothing the covers over me. At first, I tried to talk myself out of the weird feeling I was getting, but when it became very apparent that she was trying to touch me where she shouldn't, I very loudly ordered her to get out of my room. And she did. I never spoke of it to anyone."

He told her to leave. If I had done the same, maybe I could have prevented—

Mark interrupts my thoughts. "I was older than you were, N'Rama. I knew what was happening and didn't feel as obliged to obey her as I'm sure you did at your age. Don't blame yourself. What she did was disgusting and wrong no matter how you look at it. She was the adult, and she is to blame."

Embarrassed as my eyes fill with tears, I fumble to take a sip of water, listening to Pravat and Mark make idle conversation while I take a minute to compose myself.

Our food arrives, and when the waiter leaves, Mark turns to me. "I'm sorry I didn't know about all of this earlier. I would have reached out to you. I found out last night when I arrived. My father was very upset when he told me. He believes you, by the way. Even before I told him what Aunt Sunnee did to me during that trip." He smiles wanly. "I should thank you for that. I thought it was all water under the bridge, but it was very freeing telling my father about it." He lowers his eyes. "We haven't been very close, and he's ill. It broke the ice."

"Thank you for telling me about it now, P," I say sincerely. "It helps to know some of my family believes me."

"It isn't that some of them think you're a liar. It's more that they don't want to believe something so heinous about Sunnee," Mark says. "But I plan to make sure everyone knows that it happened to me, too."

"Thank you," I repeat.

As we eat, Mark's phone keeps pinging with notifications. "Sorry," he finally says, reaching into his pocket and shutting off the sound. "It's work. You'd think I could take a little time off without hearing from them." He shakes his head.

We don't talk anymore about Aunt Sunnee or what just happened at the ceremony. Instead, Mark asks about our series.

"So," he says after Pravat and I have answered his questions, "are the two of you together? I noticed you were holding hands earlier."

"We are. Off the record," Pravat says, saving me from answering. Face hot, I can only nod.

"Congratulations," Mark says. "I'm happy for you. And my lips are sealed."

When we part with him in the parking lot, I turn to Pravat and hug him.

"What's this for?" he asks softly.

"Just...for being you," I say with a sigh. When I have his arms around me, I feel like nothing else in the world exists.

CHAPTER THIRTY: Pravat

♥

Photos of Rama and I in a tight embrace standing outside the restaurant litter the bl fan sites. Evidently, a fan spotted us and went to town taking pictures on their phone. I get a call from Tida before I've had a chance to drink a cup of morning tea.

"What is this all about?" she asks, skipping a greeting.

Suddenly, I'm annoyed. Can't I comfort Rama when he needs me? Do I always have to be worried that someone is watching?

"I accompanied Rama to his cousins wedding yesterday, and there was some family trouble. Rama needed a hug."

"And you had to give it to him in public?" Tida snaps.

"P'Tida, is this really such a big deal? There are plenty of bl couples who regularly show their affection. Boss and In, for instance." It's true: that particular couple is always holding hands and hugging, spurring a lot of speculation about their relationship within the fandom.

"On the heels of Preed's accusations about you, I'd say, yes, it is a big deal. Do you want to be known as the gay bl actor, Pravat?"

"Is that so awful?" I burst out. "You'd think you were calling me a murderer or something!"

Silence. I expect Tida to ask me for confirmation on my sexuality, but she doesn't.

"Pravat, you may not realize this, but because no one wants to see them partnered with someone else, Boss and In are limited to productions they can take together. And that's okay, because they've found other ways of branding themselves. But even they don't come out and admit they're a couple off camera as well as on even though it's pretty obvious. Because that will only cause problems. Still, it's got to hurt that Boss would have been excellent in a mobster series that was recently cast, but In would not fit the character's love interest and fans will not accept Boss with anyone else. Do you want that to happen to you and Rama? Because that's where you're headed if you cultivate the idea with the press that you are a real couple."

Rubbing my eyes, I sigh heavily. I know she has a point.

"It's a little too early in the morning to have to think about this," I say.

"You should have thought about that before you wrapped your arms around Rama in a public parking lot," Tida says. Her subsequent sigh is heavier than mine. "I want to see you and Rama in my office at four. I have to go, I have another call. Please notify Rama." She disconnects, leaving me staring at my cell phone.

· ♥ · ♥ · ♥ · ♥ · ♥ ·

Rama looks cool and collected sitting beside me across from Tida's desk, but I can tell by the way he's tapping his long fingers on his leg that he's nervous. He's been tense since I told him everything Tida said to me in our earlier phone conversation.

While Tida finishes something she's working on, I scroll through the latest social media comments. They're rife with expressive stickers and emojis. Fans on Twitter are having a field day with the photos, posting them with the hashtag #PravmaIsReal.

Blbaby: Pravat holding our king! (rainbow, crown, and grumpy-face emojis)

boyskiss1000x: Out in public!!!

Exofabulous: They are a real couple. I knew it! (six red hearts)

Princess2005: What happened to Lin? (questioning face)

Exofabulous@Princess2005: Who cares? (angry and vomiting emojis)

Pravatsgrl20: Poor Lin. (unhappy face and broken heart)

PravLin@Pravatsgrl20: I keep checking her IG. She hasn't posted since the photos came out.

HotPravat31: This could just be a simple hug, people. (rolling eyes emoji)

Pravatsgrl20@HotPravat31: Simple? Do you see the look on Pravat's face? Are you BLIND?

"Pravat," Tida says, making me jerk my head up to find both her and Rama waiting patiently.

"Sorry," I say, putting away my phone.

"Have you explained the situation to Rama?"

I nod.

"I'm sorry, P'Tida," Rama says, giving her a wai. "It's my fault. I wasn't thinking."

"No, you weren't," Tida agrees sharply. "I'll be frank with you, Rama. As you know, you signed a contract with Hearts Productions on a series-by-series basis. But I was getting ready to ask you to take a part in a series playing opposite Chao Fah."

Rama frowns. "Who's that?"

I can't help but smile at how little he knows about the industry. Chao Fah Kanjanapas—or just *Fah*—is an extremely popular bl actor—one who has yet to be paired with a costar who stuck.

"This is one of the reasons why I've tried so carefully to give the impression that Pravat is dating Lin. The executives have been talking about putting the two of you together."

"Pravat and I have a lot of fans. Why mess that up?" Rama asks.

"Doing one series with Fah doesn't mean you can never work with Pravat again," Tida says. Tossing her pen on the desk, she leans back in her chair. "If you two are really in a relationship—" she holds her hand up, stopping me when I open my mouth to say something. "If you are, there can be no sign of it in your work life. I want you to think about this and get back to me. Rama, Hearts Productions would hate to lose you, but it is your choice. And as Pravat's contract is for five years, he'll be working with other people anyway and will need to keep his private life private."

"We won't let anything like what happened yesterday happen again," I assure her.

She dismisses us, and we take the elevator back down to the lobby.

Rama waits until we're in my car to turn to me and say, "I hate this. All of it." When I don't reply, he clarifies, "I don't like people controlling who I see and who I don't see,"

"It's like anyone else dating people they work with," I tell him.

Rama's laugh lacks warmth. "No, it isn't."

"You had to realize when you got into this that you'd be thrown into the spotlight," I say softly.

Sitting in the dim parking garage, we stare at each other over the console.

"I did," Rama says equally as soft. "What I didn't know was that I'd fall in love with my costar."

The car seems to heat up. "Rama. I feel the same way." My heart is beating wildly.

"Can we get out of here?" he asks.

Nodding, I hurry to start the car.

· ♥ · ♥ · ♥ · ♥ · ♥ ·

We're barely in my apartment five minutes, and I have Rama face-down on the sofa, grunting and groaning with every forceful thrust I give him. I want to consume him. Each slap of my thighs to his buttocks sends me higher until I stiffen and explode, and when I reach around to touch him, I find he's already coming.

Afterward, we lie panting, still half-dressed, without the energy to move for several long minutes.

"I don't know what to do," Rama finally says.

"Let's not talk about it until we're clean and have eaten something," I say.

We shower, kissing languidly under the water before gently washing each other. I'm completely spent, unable to do anything more even if I wanted to. We hold each other for a long time before stepping out to dry off. In the kitchen, I make some omelets and rice while Rama tidies the room. Then we watch the news while eating. It feels nice being together like this.

"We have to film two episode reactions tomorrow," Rama reminds me when we've finished eating.

"Those are usually fun," I say.

He takes our plates into the kitchen and rinses them off before coming back and settling between my legs on the couch.

"Tell me what to do," he says, looking up at me.

Running my fingers through his hair, I say, "What do you want to do? I'm behind you all the way."

"Do you really want to see me playing opposite someone else?" he asks, wrinkling his nose.

I tweak it.

"It's just a job. You'll see. What we have—that's not common." I smile at him teasingly. "Or are you afraid you're going to fall for the great Fah if you play opposite him?"

Rama frowns. "No, of course not!"

"Whoever I get paired with won't compare to you in my eyes, either. So, the question is this: Do you want to continue acting, and if so, do you want to do bl series?"

I twist a dark strand of his hair around my finger while he thinks about it.

"I love acting," he finally says. "It's what I want to do." He looks at me. "But not at the cost of losing you."

"That won't happen," I assure him.

"I'd just as soon act in bl dramas as anything else. We have that in common. But are we really going to have to sneak around in our relationship?"

"We'll only have to be discreet when we're in front of cameras," I say.

"I guess."

I smile. "You're pouting."

"I am not." Pushing my hand away from his hair, he sits up. "Let's go to bed. Maybe everything will seem easier in the morning."

CHAPTER THIRTY-ONE: Rama

The past two weeks have been weird for my family. A lot of them have stopped by the house under the guise of visiting Pah now that he's doing better, but actually to make apologies to me for their doubts. True to his word, Mark immediately told everyone about what Aunt Sunnee tried to do to him when he was seventeen, thereby corroborating my story. After a weak denial, Aunt Sunnee didn't waste time getting on a plane back to America.

The attention I've been getting from my family is embarrassing but also liberating. I finally feel as though I can let go of my past. My therapist says I'm making great strides, and I feel good about that. Maybe that's why I've been calmer lately and more confident about moving forward in both my relationship with Pravat and with work.

Due to traveling around Thailand on their honeymoon, Alex and Pete are the last to visit me, stopping by just before going to the airport to head home.

"I'm sorry. I should have whole-heartedly believed you, Rama." Pete isn't in the house two minutes before he's pulling me into a tight hug. I resist at first, but he doesn't let go, and, as I begin to relax in his embrace, the last broken shard of the hurt young boy loosens from inside me and falls away.

I shake my head. "No. I've been thinking about this, and if our roles were reversed, I don't know that I wouldn't have had doubts, too. You were being pulled from both sides and had the stress of your wedding on top of it."

Hugging me harder, Pete says, "It's nice of you forgive me so easily, especially when I didn't ask you to stand up with me at the ceremony. I regret it, now. It would have been a show of support."

I chuckle. "All I could think while you were up there was I was so glad that I wasn't. So, don't think too much about it, okay?"

Pete smiles. "Okay."

"Hey, can I get in on the hugging?" Alex teases, and Pete lets go of me so Alex can embrace me.

"Congratulations," I say to both of them. "And sorry your ceremony turned into a fiasco."

"Well, we'll certainly never forget it," Alex assures me with a grin.

We laugh, and the last of the tension dissolves.

"Don't worry. Our actual wedding in New York was wonderful." Pete pulls out his phone and spends the next fifteen minutes showing me photos of the ceremony, which really did look beautiful. I'm glad he got the special moment he deserved. When it comes time for them to leave to catch their plane, I feel good about our relationship.

Later that afternoon, as I sit looking through emails from the realtor I recently contacted about finding me an apartment, I hear Chinda return from her friend's house.

"Rama!" she yells.

"In the living room!" I call to her.

When she appears from the hall, she's frowning. "Is it true?" she asks, plopping down on the coffee table, causing me to have to save my water glass from falling.

"Is what true? Be careful!"

"I just heard a rumor that you're being considered for a series with Fah!"

"That was fast." I'd only told Tida yesterday I would do it. I haven't even met Fah yet and probably won't for a while since he is out of the country.

"But what about Pravat?" Chinda wails.

She looks so upset I can't help chuckling. "We're fine. This is a job. Did you expect me to never do another series?" I ask casually, even though it wasn't long ago that I was nearly as upset as she is about it. "The more Pravat and I discussed it, the more we realized that working with other people will make it easier to hide our relationship. And if I can get this apartment in Pravat's building that I'm looking at, all the better!"

Hand placed dramatically over her heart, Chinda sighs. "Oh! You scared me. I was afraid you guys split up."

"Never," I assure her.

Chinda grins. "My friends are driving me crazy asking about you two, but I refuse to confirm."

"Good girl." Thankfully, the necessity to keep my relationship with Pravat a secret makes my sister feel important rather than frustrated.

"Now, go away. I have to call my realtor."

Chinda rolls her eyes at me but gets up and goes into the kitchen.

· ♥ · ♥ · ♥ · ♥ · ♥ ·

Months pass. Pravat's graduation comes and goes, and social media is full of posts with pictures and commentary about the appearance I made there. All I did was walk across the lawn and hand Pravat a bouquet of flowers before sharing a hug, but from the reaction of Pravma fans, you'd think I'd dropped to one knee and confessed my undying love.

I lost the apartment in Pravat's building to someone else, but in a stroke of luck, another became available soon after, and I moved in. I wouldn't have left the house if I wasn't sure my father was going to continue allowing his subordinates to take on most of the responsibilities at work. Recently Pah has begun seeing a woman he met while he was in the hospital. I haven't seen him this happy in a long time, and she's a nurse, so she keeps him from slipping into his unhealthy ways again.

Meanwhile, Chinda has a boyfriend—someone unexpected. After breaking up with his girlfriend, Kiet began spending more time with Pravat. One night he accompanied us to Pah's house for dinner and a swim, and he and Chinda unexpectedly hit it off. I'm still not sure how I feel about it.

"Stop worrying. Kiet is respectful to her," Pravat assures me as we watch the two of them talking on a nearby park bench. After seeing a movie, we've been for a stroll. The weather is balmy, and a full moon shines above us in a cloudless sky.

"They're holding hands!" I hiss in my boyfriend's ear.

Pravat gives me a look that plainly says I'm being ridiculous. *Maybe I am*, I admit to myself grudgingly, but I protest anyway. "He just finished a long relationship. He's much more experienced than my sister. And look at that! The length of my pinky finger wouldn't fit in the space between them!"

Chuckling, Pravat wraps his arm around my shoulders and bends his head back to look up at the moon. "I've talked to him about it, and I promise everything's fine. You trust me, don't you?"

"Of course," I mutter, resting my head on his shoulder. My hand slides into Pravat's. No one's around, and this moment is private. "It's been a while since we've had time to relax together," I say.

Pravat grunts in agreement, softly squeezing my fingers.

Since the wedding, I've had to finish all the ads I'd signed up for, then Pravat had to prepare for graduation. That space between us, along with the careful way we conducted ourselves in the episode reactions we filmed, mollified Tida enough to settle her down. Plus, I've signed the contract to do the series with Chao Fah Kanjanapas, and Pravat has landed a modeling job.

Pravat seems to be thinking along the same lines as I am. "I hear you met with Fah yesterday. How did that go?"

"Well enough. He's kind of stiff," I say.

Pravat laughs. "You two have something in common, then," he says, and I thump him on the head.

Chinda's laughter rings out, and we turn to look at her and Kiet, both bent over, smiling at something on Chinda's phone. It reminds me of a subject I've been meaning to bring up with Pravat because it's going to be all over the fan sites soon.

"Guess who's been signed on as half of the secondary couple in the series?"

"Who?" Pravat asks.

"Spin! His audition was awesome!"

"Baby got a part in your series?" Pravat frowns.

"Yes! You're not excited for him?"

"To be honest, I was kind of hoping he'd give up the idea. He's so naive. I'm afraid someone will take advantage of him."

"Don't worry, I'll look after him."

Pravat nods. "Who's going to play opposite him?"

"They haven't announced it yet. I'll let you know when I hear." Thinking of Fah again, I say, "Did you say something to Fah about us?"

My suspicions are verified by Pravat's expression. "Why do you ask that?"

"You did!"

"I might have hinted that you're mine, and he'd better be respectful and take care of you."

My mouth falls open.

"I just didn't want there to be any misunderstandings, Rama, that's all."

I shake my head. "I can't believe you." Secretly, though, I'm pleased. I'm not even sure why.

Changing the subject, I say, "I hung my paintings last night." Pravat finally finished the set he'd promised me, and I love them. He painted four, each of a tree in a different season and I hung them over my couch. "You'll have to come see them."

Pravat gives me a hot look that melts me to my core.

Just then, Chinda coughs loudly, and we immediately slump down on the bench, hiding our faces as some people walk by with their dog on a leash. Pravat raises his head after they're out of sight.

"You two were in your own little world," Chinda says, coming with Kiet to stand in front of us.

"Thanks, Nong," Pravat says.

"Yeah, thanks," I echo. The last thing we need is more pictures of the two of us together, especially now that Tida seems to be softening toward our relationship, since all has been going well.

Pravat stands up and stretches, and I'm instantly distracted by the strip of tan skin between his jeans and his shirt before he lowers his arms and it disappears. Holding out his hand, he tugs me to my feet, and the four of us walk toward the lights of the parking lot.

CHAPTER THIRTY-TWO: Rama

♥

"That's a wrap!" Sun, the director of *Love Time*, barks, and Fah and I step away from each other. Finally, at the end of the third week of filming, things are settling into a productive routine. I've had a difficult time adjusting, as filming this series is so different from filming *My Doctor, My Love*. Sun is not like Maha. He's very time-conscious and inflexible when it comes to filming. One minute late, and we get a ten-minute lecture. Of course, he waits until the scene has been filmed first. And Fah. Working with him is like night and day from working with Pravat. Our first few workshops were such disasters, rumors were circulating that Tida was considering recasting our parts. I was aware of how stiff and unnatural Fah and I were with each other, but no matter how I tried, I couldn't relax enough to work on skinship with him. Luckily, two things happened that resolved the situation. First, Spin broke the ice by unexpectedly kissing his costar, Bang, during a workshop—something he didn't know he wasn't expected to actually do until he was in front of a camera. It was so shocking—he just laid one on Bang, whose face gradually turned a deep shade of red while the rest of us stared, dumbfounded. Then Fah cracked a joke, saying Spin's method of skinship was the opposite of mine, and, as we all dissolved into laughter, my reserve broke. The second thing that happened was—possibly at Tida's urging—Pravat sat me down for a talk. He reminded me that what I'm doing is a job and that I need to learn to think of Fah as a close friend, not like someone I'm cheating on Pravat with. Before that moment, I'm not sure I even realized that was how I was feeling. From that day on, I was able to loosen up, and, in turn, Fah loosened up too.

"I've never met someone so openly affectionate." Fah's comment near my ear draws my attention from studying my script. I follow his gaze to where Spin is sitting on Bang's lap on the couch. Since the day of the kiss, there have been no barriers between them. It helps that Spin's so adorable no one can resist him for long.

"It's a bit difficult for people like us to understand," I say.

Fah raises a dark brow. "People like us?"

"Yeah, you know, emotionally stilted people," I say with a grin, earning me a shove from Fah.

Recently, I got over my last hurdle when we filmed our first love scene. The night before, I tossed and turned so much Pravat threatened to go upstairs to his apartment if I didn't allow him to get some sleep before his modeling shoot the next day. As it turned out, the scene required half a dozen crew members to hover over us on the bed, holding cameras, lights, and microphones. Fah accidentally kneed me in the groin, and I almost threw up. And then I kept breaking into laughter every time he nuzzled my neck because it *tickled*, forcing us to film it at least a dozen times before I was able to get through the scene with a straight face. When I'd filmed love scenes with Pravat, all the people and equipment around us faded into the background, leaving only the two of us. But with Fah, I find I'm extremely aware of every little thing going on in the room, requiring me to rely on my skills as an actor a lot more. I've decided that's not a bad thing, as I'm honing my craft.

A stir at the other end of the room captures my attention, and I smile when I see Pravat walking toward me, looking hot as hell in a pair of dark-wash jeans ripped at the knees and a snug blue T-shirt that shows off his broad shoulders and trim waist. Tossing my script over my arm so Fah is forced to catch it, I meet Pravat half-way, wrapping my arms around him for a tight hug. A few girls in the crew titter at the sight. Thanks to Tida deciding that keeping Pravat and me happy was in the best interest of the company, our relationship is out in the open when we're at work. The silence of all Hearts Productions employees is now guaranteed by signed contract. The freedom this gives me and Pravat almost makes up for all the sneaking around and pretending we have to do in the outside world.

Spin tackles us, his small size not enough to topple us to the ground, but we stagger sideways.

"How's it going, Baby?" Pravat asks, ruffling Spin's dark hair.

"It's great! I'm having so much fun."

Pravat smiles. "I'm glad. Is Nong taking good care of you?" Pravat gestures to me.

"P'Rama is the best," Spin says loyally, eyes as bright as a puppy's.

"He's doing great," I say, earning me a grin and hug from Spin. "What are you doing here?" I ask Pravat. "I thought you had a shoot."

"We finished early, and I hoped you'd have time for lunch."

I glance toward Sun, who's talking with two of the cameramen.

"Go on. I don't think we'll be filming the next scene for a while," Fah tells me. "I just heard Sun say there's a problem with the camera they want to use."

"Okay," I said. "We'll go someplace close. Want me to bring something back for you?" I ask Fah.

"No, that's okay. I'll probably go eat with Bang and Spin."

Pravat and I descend to the first floor and walk down the street to a sandwich shop.

"How did the shoot go?" I ask him as we walk.

"It went well. I'm stiff from posing so much, though. I don't know if I'll take any more modeling jobs after this one. It's so dull and much harder than it looks."

I nod. "From the few publicity shoots we've done, I would imagine it is."

"And it's not as fun without you," Pravat adds.

I smile. We're walking with a good three feet between us, being careful not to seem anything more than friends, not that anyone seems to be watching us. But you never know.

After we order our food, Pravat says, "P'Tida has a role for me."

"She does?"

He nods. "Production will start in a couple of months, giving me time to wrap up this modeling job."

"What's the series?" I ask, pushing down the uncomfortable feeling rising in my gut.

"To be honest, I can't remember the name. She only told me about it this morning on the phone. What I'm more excited about is working with the director, Banlop Suprija."

"Yeah? Why's that?"

"He's legendary and only recently started working with Hearts Productions. I'm eager to see his techniques."

"You'd make an awesome director, Pravat," I say, meaning it. He's so patient and pays such great attention to detail. We've discussed this a lot lately, and each time, I think Pravat believes in himself a little more.

He smiles. "Thanks. Right now, I don't know, but this feels like the right step for me. If I can learn a few things from Banlop Suprija, I just might decide to pursue directing."

"So, uh, do you know who you'll be playing opposite?" I ask.

"Yeah. Two."

"Two?" I ask, surprised.

Pravat nods. "Does that bother you?"

"It would be a little hypocritical of me to protest, don't you think?"

Pravat chuckles. "Maybe, but that doesn't answer the question."

I sigh. "Sure. It's your job, and I know better than anyone it isn't a big deal. Honestly, I think the fact that it's Two makes it easier." I laugh. "Better him than Mint, right?"

"Hell, yes," Pravat says, laughing with me.

Pravat changes the subject, telling me about his recent appointment with his therapist. He's making headway in his lingering grief and issues from the past, and that makes me so happy.

On our way back to the studio, a couple of fans approach us, phones held up, telling us they are filming.

"P'Rama! P'Pravat! Are you two working together again?" the boy asks.

Before we can answer, the girl with him says, "I thought P'Rama was filming a series with P'Fah?"

We smile and answer their questions, telling them we were having a friendly lunch to catch up with each other, when in reality, we spend every night in each other's arms. The subterfuge is sort of thrilling. Maybe it will keep our relationship new and fresh as time moves on.

Any way I look at it, life is good. It may not be exactly the way I pictured it three years ago, but in a lot of aspects, it's much better. I have the career I wanted, and I've finally put away the awful memories that have tortured me for years, although I suspect I'll continue therapy for some time. I may work long hours, but at night I have someone to snuggle up to who makes me feel like no one else ever has.

For the first time, I can relate to my name.

Rama.

King of my world.

THE END

Acknowledgements

Thank you for reading my new boys' love series! Although different from my other series, I have immensely enjoyed writing these books and plan to continue as long as there are readers enjoying them. A heart-felt apology to anyone from Thailand who may have noticed errors or inconsistencies.

Expect Spin's book late 2023, early 2024.

Follow me on Bookbub

Follow me on Amazon

Join my Facebook Readers' Group

Subscribe to my newsletter for release news and boys' love fun

Also By Rebecca James

Shifter/Mpreg Series

The River Wolf Pack Series
First Omega
Second Alpha
Third Mate

The Angel Hills Series
Omega Arrival
Ripples of Threat
Winter's End

The Cascade City Series
New Beginnings
Breaking the Bonds
Running Free

Omegaverse Mpreg

SOS Series

The Alpha's Forbidden Omega
The Alpha's Unexpected Omega

Sci-fantasy Mpreg

Teresias Bound
The Wolves of Daos 5

Non-Mpreg Contemporary

Partners

The Hedonist Series

The Ballerino and the Biker
The Pet Stylist and the Playboy
The Brat and the Bossman
The Survivor and his Safe Place
The Hacker and his Heart's Desire
The Diva and his Daddy
The Single Dad and his Soulmate
The Hookup and the Hedonist

The Balls and Brawn Series

Wanna Bet? (prelude short story)
Out of Harm's Way (Book 1)
All Bets are Off (Book 2)
Out of Reach (Book 3)

The Just Friends Series

Love Eventually
Wrapped in Red

The Boys' Love Series

Boys' Love (Pravat and Rama)
In Love (part 2 Pravat and Rama)
Baby Love (Spin's story)

Printed in Great Britain
by Amazon